Sudden
Mission

By
Guy L. Pace

Copyright © 2015 Guy L. Pace

Cover Design by Scott Deyett

Edited by Brandi Midkiff

This is a work of fiction. Names, characters, places, brands, media, and incidents are either the product of the author's imagination or are used fictitiously. Any resemblance to similarly named places or to persons living or deceased is unintentional.

ISBN-10: 0-9978669-0-X
ISBN-13: 978-0-9978669-0-2

Library of Congress Control Number: 2015948638

Acknowledgements

I want to thank Michelle Bellon and Nadine Brandes for their early reads, edits, encouragements, and helps. I also want to especially thank the members of my Vox Dei team; Heather Huffman, Kathy Marks, Brandi Midkiff, Scott Deyett, and Sophie Thomas, for their hard work, incredible talent, and for believing in the project. Of course, all the glory goes to God.

*To Connie, my first reader
and primary support system.*

CHAPTER ONE

Coyote

PAUL RAN.

Breathing steadily, he felt the grip of his shoes on the track as he rounded the sweeping curve. Behind him he could hear the rhythmic pace of the other boys behind him. A couple of them kicked up for the last stretch of the long mile.

Paul Shannon owned this distance, though. His favorite run. And it couldn't be more perfect in the clear, late spring North Carolina morning. The smell of green, growing things filled the air and the intense blue canopy of the Carolina sky.

Paul waited a few more seconds, then poured on his final kick. He stretched out his stride and dug harder against the surface of the track. His breath remained steady, and he heard the labored breathing of another boy off to one side. That boy started to fall back.

Another runner surged up and tried to stay with Paul and actually came along his right side, but Paul's speed and strength were just too much. He dropped back as well. Paul cruised across the finish line where the physical education teacher marked time.

"Good run, Paul," he said.

"Thanks, coach," Paul said breathlessly, and then slowed to a lope. He continued around again, cooling down. He felt good. A mile, a bit over four minutes, at a measured pace with a strong finish always put him in a good mood.

He didn't have any competition in his freshman class. Even at the local invitational meets, his best competition came from high school seniors or from the local colleges. He liked those competitions. They made him work for the wins, made him try harder.

Next week's invitational meet at Chapel Hill filled his head with ideas and strategies as he jogged down the back straight of the track. Then something in the trees nearby caught his eye. Gray and tan, it slipped in and out of the trees, then kept pace with Paul, matching his easy stride. A coyote.

Paul had heard of coyotes being seen around his town before, but this one came pretty close to him. It had the classic narrow face and snout, gangly legs, and furry tail. He'd never heard of them being aggressive or attacking humans, though they did snatch neighborhood cats, small dogs, and other small animals. This one just matched Paul's pace and watched him.

Paul slowed, wondering what the coyote would do. It turned back into the trees. As it did it looked back at Paul and a deep red, fiery glow shown in its eyes. Then it was gone.

He stopped and watched the spot where the coyote had vanished. The memory of the red, glowing eyes sent a tingle of unease down his spine.

Weird, he thought. What would a coyote be doing around here?

Shouts and loud voices across the field brought Paul back to the here and now.

"Hit the showers!" the teacher yelled. "You have ten minutes. Anyone late does an extra five laps next time."

#

"What were you doing over there?" Joe Banes asked Paul as they toweled off and dressed by their lockers. Paul looked at his best friend. "You were staring off into the trees. Thought maybe you were about to hurl."

Paul stood a half-head taller than Joe, who had a stockier build with the heavy shoulders of a football player. Joe had an open, honest face with chocolate-brown eyes and wide mouth.

Paul slipped his shirt over his head and pulled it down. "I was looking at a coyote. It ran with me a bit, then disappeared. I was just trying to see if I could see where it went."

Joe's dark brown, arrow-straight hair stuck out in all directions and he tried to hand-comb it down. "Maybe it wanted to race."

Paul smiled, then frowned. "Yeah, I don't know. Its eyes sorta glowed." Paul stood and ran the towel through his soft, curly black hair one more time. "Gave me the willies."

"Probably a trick of the light. Like when you get red-eye in a picture."

"Probably."

Dressed and with their backpacks, they stood in front of a mirror. Joe took a couple more swipes at his shock of wild, straight hair before heading to their next class.

Amy Grossman met them in the halls. The third member of their tribe, Amy stood just a little taller than the two boys and wore her abundant auburn hair long and tied back. Paul liked to think of her gray eyes as dancing and sparkling above those freckled cheeks. Of course, Paul wouldn't say anything like that aloud. While he focused on running, Amy studied martial arts and could probably lay both him and the more powerfully built Joe out flat with little effort.

"Paul kicked everyone's behind in the mile again today," Joe said.

"So, what's new about that?" Amy tossed up her hands.

"Geez." Paul smiled.

"And he saw a coyote."

"Really? Where?" she asked.

"Out on the other side of the track." Paul pointed with his thumb in the general direction. "He ran along with me for a bit."

"Huh!" Amy said. "Unusual."

"And it had devilish, glowing eyes!" Joe said, flailing his fingers to imitate flames coming out of his own eyes.

"Oh, knock it off." Paul gave Joe a gentle nudge on the shoulder. "They seemed to glow just before it turned back into the trees. Probably just a trick of the light."

"Well, I wouldn't want one that close to me," Amy said. "You never know, it may have rabies. Was it foaming at the mouth?"

"No."

"It just had fire coming out of its eyes," Joe said. "He's lucky it didn't shoot rays and burn his face off." Joe covered his face with his hands and stumbled around as though struck blind. Amy rolled her eyes.

"Get to class!" a teacher on hall monitor duty told them. "Drama club meets next week, Banes. Keep a lid on it until then."

CHAPTER TWO

Troubles

PAUL MET Amy and Joe after classes for the walk home. Warm air from the late spring afternoon hit them as they left the school building. Amy lived just around the block from Paul, and Joe's house was a block past her house.

"I've been thinking about that coyote you saw on the track this morning," Amy said. "Coyotes aren't usually that bold. We rarely ever see them up close. I wonder what's driving them into town?"

"True," Joe said. "I've never heard of one coming up like that. Of course, Paul is the only one who saw it."

They were all silent for a bit.

"I heard of some cats going missing, too," Amy said. "I'm going to ask my dad tonight. He might know something."

"Okay," Paul said. He kicked a small pebble on the path and it tumbled into the stream they were about to cross on a small wooden bridge. "Let us know what he says when we get online tonight."

"I have a lot of homework." Joe shifted his pack on his shoulders. "I may get online a little late."

"We won't log on to the game without you," Paul said.

He waved as Joe and Amy headed off to their houses.

#

"I'm home," Paul said as he came through his front door.

A laughing yell from his baby brother was the only response, as the four-year-old launched himself into Paul's arms.

"Hey there, Roger Rabbit!" Paul said, hugging the little bundle of energy and setting him back down. "How you been?"

"I good. S'rah 'n Momma inna kitchen!" Roger said and disappeared into the family room.

Paul set his pack by the stairs and entered the kitchen. His mother was glued to the news on the flat-screen TV in the kitchen and his little sister, Sarah, was working on something involving paper and crayons at the kitchen table. He expected to be ignored by Sarah, but his mother usually gave him a hug and asked about his day when he got home. He looked at the TV.

"Nation's capital blanketed by black fog," read the video headline as a newscaster described the day's events.

"A black fog descended on the metropolitan area of Washington, D.C., this morning," the newscaster said. "All vehicle traffic is stopped at the wall of fog and no one and no communication is coming from inside the fog. Local police are trying to keep everyone back and struggling to reroute traffic around the city." She looked seriously out at the audience. "The fog built up to a height of more than two hundred feet and covered the Pentagon on the south side and extends outside the Beltway all around the city." Camera shots appeared over her shoulder on the screen and displayed stalled traffic and the flashing lights of emergency vehicles on I-395 just before a boiling black wall of fog.

"Hi, honey," Paul's mom finally said, still glued to the newscast. Her silky black hair was tied up with a colorful scarf and she dabbed at her dark brown eyes with a tissue. "Go do your homework. We'll have dinner when Dad gets home."

Paul, concerned by the news, stayed by the kitchen entry and watched the television.

"There is no word from Congress or the president," the newscaster continued. "The secretary of state, who was traveling, is on her way to Denver. At this time, she seems to be the most senior member of the government not affected by today's events. Other members of government are trying to reach the Denver emergency site to establish communication and control." The screen then switched to a street reporter who was interviewing some people in Alexandria.

"It has to be a new Russian weapon," one man told the reporter.

"It's Armageddon," a woman said. "I'm a psychic. I predicted this last week."

Paul grabbed his pack and went up to his room. He worked on his homework assignments until he heard his father come in the door. Paul's dad wasn't one to raise his voice, but Paul could hear him as he entered the kitchen. Could he be talking about the newscast? Paul left his books and went downstairs.

"I heard on the radio that flying saucers landed near Hyderabad, India," his dad said as Paul walked into the kitchen. His briefcase lay on the kitchen counter and that was another thing Paul never saw his father do. His mom insisted it be put on the floor.

His parents stood at the kitchen counter. Dad had an arm around Mom's shoulders. His gray eyes followed everything on the screen, and occasionally he ran his free hand through his bushy brown hair as the newscasters shifted from one story to another.

A TV report showed Mexico City in a whiteout blizzard, buried in six feet of snow. The next shot was in London, England, where temperatures had reached 110 degrees and sick and dying elderly people flooded the hospitals. In Paris, France, the camera showed frogs covering the ground at the Eiffel Tower. Los Angeles, California, from the next stream of videos, seemed to have the worst of it. Earthquakes repeatedly shook the region, tsunamis washed ashore and wiped out whole communities, and fires raged in the hills surrounding the city.

While everyone was engrossed in the news reports, Paul picked up his little brother and set him in his chair at the table. He served up some tuna casserole and a salad his mom had prepared for dinner for himself and Roger, then sat in his usual spot and prayed grace for the food.

"Aren't you going to wait for Mom and Dad?" Sarah asked, wrinkling her freckled nose at him.

"Strange things are going on. I think they'll be glued to the news for a while." Paul pushed the casserole dish toward her. "If you don't want to starve, I recommend you eat, too."

"I won't starve," she said, and went back to what she was working on.

"Moscow has a white fog covering it," his mom said. "How strange! Our capital gets black fog, and the Russians get white."

"It must all be random, then," his dad said. "Nothing on this channel about Hyderabad. The radio said something about aliens blasting everything in sight there. They're probably laying waste to the entire region."

The newscast broke with a "more at eleven" message, and his parents came to the table and dished up their own plates.

"Stuff like that has been reported all day," his mom said.

"Speaking of weird things," Paul said, "I saw a coyote this morning, and he ran with me for a ways."

"That's nice, dear." His mom smiled at Paul. Her eyes were red-rimmed.

"A what?" his dad said around a mouthful of the casserole.

"A coyote."

"What did it do?"

"I had just finished a mile run, and I was cooling down. The coyote came out of the woods on the far side of the track and ran alongside me for about a hundred meters. Then it disappeared."

"Did it do anything?" His dad looked carefully at Paul.

"Just ran along."

"So it didn't try to bite you or anything?"

"No, but--"

Paul stopped. The red, glowing eyes probably were just a trick of the light. His parents were worried enough about what was going on in the world; he didn't need to add to it.

"But what?" Dad asked.

"Well, nothing. It just followed me and looked at me. Nothing like that ever happened before."

Dad nodded and went back to his food.

Sarah started repeating what she had heard on the television, counting off the events on her fingers. She ran out of fingers. Roger, the copycat, started counting, too.

"One, three, five, two," he said holding up his fingers, then ate another bite of the casserole.

"Never mind, dear. Let the adults worry about this." Mom patted Sarah's hands.

Paul finished his meal in silence, then excused himself. Up in his room, he launched his video call application on the computer and rang for Amy and Joe. There was no response for a bit, then Amy connected. A window appeared on his screen with her solemn face inside.

"Did you hear about the things going on?" Paul asked her.

"Yes. It's really weird. Scary."

Joe popped up, his face showing up in another window on Paul's screen.

"Hey," he said. "Man, there is some strange stuff going on!"

"Hmm," Amy said, her face turned to the side in her window. "I'm pulling up a list of the strange events. There are hundreds. One place, a city called Goiania in Brazil, just disappeared."

"What?" Joe said.

"Yes," Amy said. "It just disappeared. The story is a little confusing, though. Something lost in the translation, I bet."

Paul focused on his own browser and typed in a search string. After a moment, he had a listing, as well. He scanned down through it.

"This is more than 'wars and rumors of wars,'" Paul said, "What's the reference?"

"That's Mark thirteen, seven through nine," Joe said. "Got it here: *When you hear of wars and rumors of wars, do not be alarmed. Such things must happen, but the end is still to come. Nation will rise against nation, and kingdom against kingdom. There will be earthquakes in various places, and famines. These are the beginning of birth pains. You must be on your guard. You will be handed over to the local councils and flogged in the synagogues. On account of me you will stand before governors and kings as witnesses to them.*"

"Los Angeles has been hit with a lot of earthquakes," Paul said. "And fire and tidal waves."

"But how do the white fog and black fog, disappearing cities, and all this other stuff fit into that?" Amy asked. "And aliens. I heard aliens landed in some places. There must be something else going on. This can't be what Jesus talked about. Can it?"

"It seems kind of random to me," Paul said. "It doesn't seem to fit the prophecy of the end times, but it sure is getting attention. I certainly don't want to get flogged in a synagogue."

Joe rubbed his face. "I'm having trouble believing all this. We aren't seeing anything really close to us, so it's hard to relate."

"Yeah," Paul said. "It's almost like we're seeing a low budget SF movie on TV, but no cheesy special effects." He saw Amy looking away from her window. "What do you have there?"

"Just more reports," Amy said looking back. "They're coming in from all over. Except for China. They don't give out much. But similar things like strange weather, cities disappearing, earthquakes, fogs, plagues of frogs, snakes, and spiders, huge waves and tides."

"All from news outlets, right? None of those fake news sites."

"No, no fake news sites," she said. "All primary sources like Reuters and Associated Press."

"Well, it isn't biblical," Paul said. "Something has gone wrong. Seriously wrong."

"Yeah," Joe nodded.

"Well, I think we should pray about this," Amy said.

The three prayed together online. They asked for help and understanding, and for strength in dealing with whatever was behind it all. Amy closed with a request for blessings for those suffering during these troubles.

Homework done, they launched into their online role-playing game. Even after finding some important treasures and artifacts in the game, and each of them leveling up and gaining new skills, their hearts weren't in it. They logged out early. Paul went to bed and fought to get to sleep. Images from the TV and his imagination flowed through his thoughts.

CHAPTER THREE

Angel

PAUL JERKED awake. The morning sun poured through his bedroom window and flooded his room in light. He'd overslept and would be late to school.

He scrambled out of bed, got into the bathroom and showered.

It wasn't until he'd washed, brushed, and dressed that he realized no one had bothered him today. No Roger Rabbit, no Sarah. No Mom hollering up the stairs for him to hurry and get breakfast.

He glanced out his room's window. No car in the driveway.

A small pit of panic formed inside. He grabbed his pack and charged down the stairs.

A Danish on a small plate on the kitchen table held down a note. He looked around to see if anyone was still around. Mornings at the Shannon household were normally messy and chaotic. But today the whole house looked clean, at least what Paul could see of it.

"Paul," the note read, "we had to go into Charlotte to visit Aunt Grace. She is in the hospital. We'll be back in a few days. Sorry. There is plenty to eat in the fridge and freezer. You're a big boy, you can deal with this. Love, Mom and Dad."

He sat on a stool as he took this in. Aunt Grace, his mom's sister, was in poor health, Paul knew. But taking off to Charlotte without him, without even saying goodbye, leaving no more than a note and a Danish? Was that even legal? Yes, he could deal with it, but this wasn't the sort of thing his parents did.

He was late and didn't have time to figure this out now. He opened the fridge and grabbed a small milk bottle, then ripped off a paper towel and grabbed the Danish. Out the door, he wolfed down the pastry and gulped the milk as he headed to school. It was a good thing he was never tardy, he told himself. He shouldn't get detention for this one time.

Wait. Paul stopped a moment. Why hadn't Joe and Amy come by? They always walked together. He looked around the neighborhood. He was alone.

He crossed the small bridge on the path and a man appeared alongside him. Paul walked quickly, but the man kept up with an easy gait.

"Hello, Paul," the man said.

Chills ran down Paul's back. He'd never seen this man before.

"Who are you?" Paul asked around a mouthful of Danish.

"I'm a friend," the man said.

Paul looked more closely. The man was . . . beautiful. That wasn't something he would normally say to describe a man, but this guy had a face that looked like it came from Michelangelo's statue of David. Paul had trouble getting a read on what the man wore. At one point, he wore a nice business suit. At next glance, he wore robes. Paul started to do double and triple takes, but when the robes gave way to a clown costume he felt a bit dizzy and focused on the man's face.

"I don't know you," Paul said as he gulped down the last of the milk and shoved the small plastic bottle into a pocket in his pack. "I shouldn't talk to you. And I'm late." He stepped up his pace, almost running now.

"No, you don't know me. You do know my boss, though. You are chosen. And I have a message for you."

"A message? From your boss? Who's that?"

"The Lord God. Well, actually, it is a mission."

Paul stopped. The strange man stopped beside him. Paul pinched his own arm. Either this guy was a real creeper, or Paul was still in bed and dreaming.

"A mission?"

"Yes."

"Who is your boss, again?"

"God. The Almighty. The Magnificent! The Alpha and the Omega." The man's face beamed with wonder and adoration.

"What is this mission?"

"You are to travel to Choteau, Montana to do something that will restore the world."

"What am I supposed to do?"

"That I do not know. I am just the messenger."

"Look, I'm fourteen. I can't drive and I don't even know how to get to Montana. How am I supposed to get there and do this thing?"

Paul stopped. How much information should he give this stranger? He turned and continued walking.

"I am just the messenger, Paul."

"I have to get to school, now. I'm already late," he said, pointing toward the school. The building was still about a block away. "How can God ask me to do something like this?"

Paul turned, but the strange man was gone. And when he turned back again, he found that he was standing right at the front door of the school.

#

"What happened to you this morning?" Joe asked when he caught up to Paul at lunch break.

"My folks went to Charlotte and just left me a note," he said as they entered the school cafeteria.

"You're kidding! My folks went to Charlotte, too! They woke me up early and told me they were going to see my grandma at the hospital there."

Paul looked at Joe. Joe's parents, too? At least they'd woken him up. He got a tray from the stack and started through the food line. Joe held his tray up and watched as a server plopped some meat on it.

"Mine just left me a note and a Danish," Paul said, getting a similar plop of food on his tray. "And on the way to school, this man talked to me."

"Who?"

"I don't know. He said I was chosen and had a mission."

"Did he look like Tom Cruise? Is it a *Mission: Impossible*?"

"No. Well, maybe. But, he was . . . I don't know how to say this. He was beautiful, you know? But I can't describe what he was wearing. It changed all the time."

They sat at a table. Their trays had meatloaf, potatoes, peas and pudding.

"God, bless this food. It needs it. Please don't let it poison us," Joe prayed in earnest.

"Amen," Amy said as she joined them at the table. "My parents left this morning for Charlotte. They have to visit my grandpa in the hospital."

Paul and Joe froze with forks full of meatloaf and mouths open.

"All our parents left for Charlotte this morning? And all for relatives in the hospital?" Paul said. "That can't be a coincidence."

As they ate, Paul told the story about the strange man, this time in a bit more detail.

"This is insane," he said in conclusion. "How would I get to Montana and do whatever it is? Why would I be chosen? I'm nobody, just a kid. That dude must be playing some kind of crazy joke."

"A joke that included instant transport to the front door of the school from over a block away?" said Joe.

Paul frowned. "That part doesn't make any sense. *None* of it makes any sense. Maybe I imagined the whole thing."

"I've never known you to be prone to illusions," Amy said. "You have a pretty firm grip on reality."

The three posed and discarded theories throughout the rest of the lunch period, but came up with nothing that seemed to make sense.

Later, in physical education class, Paul again saw the coyote during his cool-down lap after the mile. This time, it paused and stared hard at Paul. Then its eyes glowed like red coals and it disappeared into the trees as it had before.

Paul stood stunned. When the coyote had stared at him, he'd felt buffeted by some dark force, unable to move or fight back, like in a bad dream. The feeling had lessened when the coyote vanished, but he still felt weak, lost, breathless, hopeless.

He sat on the edge of the track afterward to collect himself. Something seemed broken inside. *Helpless and hopeless*, he thought.

"What's the matter?" Joe asked, running up to him. "Are you okay?"

"Yeah," Paul said. "I'm okay. I saw the coyote again. Did you see him?"

"No. I just saw you standing here, then saw you sit down. Coach had me back there doing wind sprints."

"You didn't see the coyote?" Paul asked again, wishing for some confirmation, something that would shore up his sanity.

"No. I didn't see anything."

Paul pointed at the trees, where the coyote had stood and stared. "He was right there. You didn't see him?"

"No."

"Oh, crap," Paul said. His parents were off to Charlotte and he was losing his mind.

"It's okay, Paul. C'mon, get up."

"It's not okay." He stood, feeling a little wobbly, and reached for Joe for support. "It's not okay if I'm starting to hallucinate."

#

Paul walked home with Amy and Joe, as usual, but he was quiet. He felt strange, lost, since the meeting with the coyote that afternoon, but glad for the company of his best friends.

"What should we do for dinner?" Paul asked. "I don't want to spend the entire evening alone."

"Well, let's go to your house. We can study there," Amy said. "I need to stop at my house first, then I'll come over. We can find something for dinner. I'll make something quick and fun."

"Sounds like a plan," Joe said. "I need to run over to my house first, too."

They turned down the path that led to their neighborhood and stopped in their tracks. The small wooden bridge across the stream, the bridge they'd crossed every day for years, was gone. In its place was a larger stone bridge.

And standing in front of the bridge, blocking their way, was a large, hulking, gray-skinned thing. It had long, stringy, oily-looking hair, a huge nose with bumps, and arms so long the hands hung below its knees. Its mouth was wide with irregular teeth and large, loose lips. It drooled.

"What's that?" Joe said.

"It's . . . it's a troll," Paul said.

CHAPTER FOUR

Troll

"A TROLL?" Amy said. "How . . . I haven't heard of any trolls on the news."

"I don't know," Paul said. He could see a bit of blurring around the area, about twenty feet to each side. "Don't get too close, though. This scene has . . . edges."

"I don't think we want to cross that stone bridge, either," Amy said. "I doubt we'll find our homes over there."

Joe shook his head. "I don't think we can just ignore this one like we do the trolls in our online forums."

The troll looked the three over carefully. It licked its large lips with a gray, slimy tongue, and smiled.

"You tasty morsels will be mine, unless you can answer my riddle."

A troll with a riddle, Paul thought. *Just more evidence the world has gone insane. Or I have.*

"That's what trolls do in fairy tales," Paul said, taking a tentative step forward. "Who are you and why are you blocking our way?"

"This," the troll said, waving his gnarled hand, "is my bridge. If you wish to cross, you must pay my tax. My tax is the answer to a riddle. Answer the riddle, you cross. Fail, and you fill my stew pot."

"Okay, troll," Joe said, stepping up beside Paul. "Tell us the riddle."

"When I tell the riddle, you get one chance to answer correctly. Fail and you are stew. Do you agree?" The troll's tongue licked out across his flabby lips again.

Paul looked at the other two. Amy, a dangerous determination burning in her eyes, nodded. So did Joe. Paul made a curt nod then Amy stepped forward.

"Tell the riddle, troll," Amy said.

The troll took one step forward, smiled his crooked smile, and licked his lips again. Drool dripped from his slack jaw.

"Here is the riddle," he said. "One kissed Heaven's door, but now burns in Hell."

Paul stepped next to Amy and turned to his friends, keeping an eye on the troll. "We get one shot here," he said.

"You'd think I'd know this," Amy said, "but I'm stumped."

Paul never liked riddles. He took statements at face value and found it difficult to look beneath the surface for meaning. *Think*, he told himself.

"How do you kiss Heaven's door and end up in Hell?" he said softly to the others.

"The key is Heaven's door," Joe said, then started humming the tune to "Knocking on Heaven's Door."

The troll stepped closer.

"It's a good song, Joe, but I doubt it's relevant," Paul said. "And the humming isn't helping."

Joe stopped humming.

"Heaven's door," Amy whispered, more to herself but loud enough for Paul and Joe to hear. "*I am the way and the truth and the life. No one comes to the Father except through me.* John fourteen something. Jesus is Heaven's door."

The troll took another step closer.

"I think you're getting warmer," Joe said, watching the troll.

"So you kiss Heaven's door and end up in Hell," Paul said. "You kiss Jesus and . . . got it."

Paul spun to face the troll. "Back off! We have the answer to your riddle."

The troll took a step back and wiped his arm across his mouth. "One chance. Fail and you are stew!"

"Judas Iscariot betrayed Jesus with a kiss," Paul said. "In self-loathing he hanged himself and now burns in Hell. Jesus is Heaven's Door."

The troll's eyes grew wide, then it stomped around in anger, shouting, "No stew! No stew! No stew!" Finally, the troll and the scene disappeared with a flash and roiling clouds of smoke. When the smoke cleared, they saw the familiar small wooden bridge. An acrid, sulfurous stench lingered in the air.

"Let's get across before something else happens," Joe said.

#

Paul got a water bottle from the fridge. He'd reached home without any other incidents, but he still had an overwhelming foreboding. He kept flashing back to the encounters with the coyote and the troll. Added to that, the strange man's claim that he'd been chosen and assigned a mission continued to churn in his head.

Choteau, Montana. Paul couldn't conceive of how he would get there. He had looked up the small Montana town on a computer at school. It was a long way from his home near Raleigh, North Carolina. All his earlier objections were legitimate: too young, no driving, too far. And, really, just who was this stranger, anyway? Why should Paul believe him? Paul didn't know many people outside his family, friends, and church. He considered taking this to one of his pastors or an elder.

He went to the kitchen phone and was scanning the church directory for elders when the doorbell rang. He hesitated. Should he answer it? It was too early for Amy and Joe. The bell rang again. He approached the door carefully, then called out, "Who is it?"

"Paul, I'd like to speak with you."

Paul recognized the voice of the strange man. "What do you want?"

"I want to speak with you."

"What if I don't want to speak with you?"

"That is easily solved." The strange man filtered through the door. Paul scrambled backward and fell. "I only rang the bell to be courteous."

He looked the same as he had earlier in the day, beautiful, but with clothing that seemed to shift with thought. Again, Paul tried to focus on the man's face and ignore the clothing.

"I didn't invite you," Paul said, getting up off the floor.

"I've been sent," the man said. "I worship the Creator, Almighty God, and do his bidding. You need to go to Choteau, Montana."

"How am I supposed to do that?"

"You only have to choose to do as your Creator asks. The Lord God provides. I do not know how the task is to be accomplished. I am just the messenger."

"You said that before. I don't get this," Paul said. "This has to be some kind of joke. Who would ask a 14-year-old to travel twenty-five hundred miles to find or do something? What could I do that would restore the world from all these strange events?"

"I'm sorry, Paul, I don't have all the answers for you. I am simply a messenger. Only God, the Everlasting, Who Was and Is and Is to Come, knows the answers."

"Well, I've got a lot more questions. What are my folks doing in Charlotte? Why was there a troll blocking the bridge on the way home? And what's the deal with that red-eyed coyote?"

"A coyote?" the man interrupted. He moved closer and gazed into Paul's eyes. "Ah! Yes, I see."

He reached out his hands to hold Paul's head. Paul tried to pull away, but the man's hold was firm. Paul closed his eyes, afraid and hopeful at the same time.

"Begone!" The man's voice was soft yet reverberated through him.

Paul felt his entire body and soul vibrate. Something cleansing flowed through him. The man's hands released him and Paul opened his eyes. The dark foreboding had vanished.

"Yes, he is gone," the man said, looking deeply into Paul's eyes.

"What did you do?"

"I may be a simple messenger, but I can turn away the Adversary or one of his minions," the man said. "He left a cloud over your soul. I removed it. You should feel better now."

"Yes, I do." Paul legs felt rubbery and he sat down on the stairs. "Who are you? Do you have a name?"

"I am one who serves and worships God, Father and Son and Holy Spirit. I have no name as you understand it. However, I have been called Gabriel."

"Gabriel?" Paul looked at him narrowly. "You're an angel." This got stranger by the minute.

"Yes," Gabriel said, "my kind are also called angels."

"But you're supposed to blow the horn that announces the return of Jesus."

"That is a figurative description of one of my roles, yes, but that time has not yet come."

"That's comforting."

"So, back to the original issue. We need you to go to Choteau."

"Again, how can I, a fourteen-year-old who cannot drive, go that far? Why me?" He stood and stepped closer to Gabriel. "Did you have something to do with our parents going to Charlotte?"

"No. I think the Adversary may have manipulated that. Look, Paul, I watched Moses fret and fume when God commanded him to return to Egypt. Still, he went and God provided. You have been chosen. God has laid a mission on your heart. He will, in His infinite wisdom and capacity, provide."

Paul suddenly felt the weight of the mission, the burden of the responsibility, and the loving touch of God on his heart. He knew he could not refuse. He would accept. He would go.

"So what do I have to do to accomplish this mission?"

"You must go."

"Now?"

"Yes. Time is short. The Adversary is moving."

CHAPTER FIVE

Travel

PAUL PULLED the books and school materials from his backpack and tossed them on the bed. *What a messed up world*, he thought as he dug through his dresser and closet for a few changes of clothing and an extra pair of athletic shoes. Some of the things that were going on seemed pretty serious. Was there any relationship between what happened to a particular city and the kind of wickedness that city held? Still, weren't good people in those places as well? The sheer numbers of lives lost so far overwhelmed him.

His tablet slid into the padded sleeve with the power adapter tucked alongside. His parents didn't spend the money for the extra phone network, so the tablet only had wireless capability. That was enough for Paul, though, and the tablet would be handy for accessing information where Wi-Fi was available. He moved things around a bit to make room for some other supplies.

He pulled an old shoe box from under his bed. Inside was his stash of allowance and last summer's lawn-mowing money. It amounted to just over two hundred dollars. He shoved the bills in his jeans pockets, slung the pack over his shoulder, and went downstairs.

Food. He went through the cupboards for lightweight food. *This isn't going to work very well*, he thought, as he looked at the huge economy-sized boxes of cereal and bags of trail mix, cookies, and other things. Small plastic bags, that was the ticket! He opened a drawer and grabbed a handful of resealable plastic sandwich bags. Vanilla cookies in one. Trail mix in four. Then the doorbell rang.

Now what? He went to the door. Gabriel had disappeared as soon as Paul had accepted the mission and started packing, so he shouldn't be back so soon.

"Who's there?" he called out.

"Joe and Amy," said Joe's voice.

Relieved, he opened the door. The two stood there dressed for trekking, with backpacks loaded.

"What are you doing?" Paul asked.

Joe's eyes widened in mock astonishment. "What do you mean, what are we doing? You invited us for dinner, remember?"

"Actually, I think you invited yourselves. But why are you all geared up?"

"We were on the way over for dinner, and this man told us you were leaving. He said you would need help," Amy said. "So we went back and packed up. Here we are."

"Did he say where I'm heading or how I'm supposed to get there?"

"No, just that you would need our help," Joe said. "So here we are. Big duh!"

"I think it was the man you told us about," Amy said hugging herself. "He was gorgeous! But I see what you mean about the clothing. The constant changing made me dizzy."

"Dizzier than usual . . . " Joe started. "Ouch!" He rubbed his shoulder where Amy punched him.

Paul's throat felt tight. "Thanks, guys. It'll be nice not having to do it all alone."

Joe and Amy smiled. They all stood there awkwardly for a moment. Then Paul said briskly, "Come on, let's make some sandwiches. They won't last long, but they'll get us through the first couple of days."

Paul got out turkey, ham, and cheese from the fridge and they made several sandwiches, loading them carefully in the top of the packs. Amy grabbed bananas, wrapped each in paper towels, and squirreled them around in the smaller spaces.

"Water?" she asked.

Paul pointed to the pantry. Amy came out with several bottles of water. These were shoved into bottle sleeves and other places on the packs. Then she gave a bottle to each of the boys.

"Drink now," she said. "Use the bathroom. No telling when we'll get another chance."

In the meantime, Paul got out some leftover casserole and heated it in the microwave. They ate quickly, used the bathroom as needed. Then Paul grabbed a ring of house keys and turned off lights. They went through the front door, and Paul locked it behind them.

#

"Okay," Paul said after about fifteen minutes of hiking toward a main road that would take them to the freeway. "The man . . . I think he's Gabriel. You know, the angel, the messenger."

He looked at the others. Were they buying this? Both looked back at him, Amy with wide eyes.

"I'm not crazy," Paul said.

"No one said you were," Joe said, "no one with any credentials, anyway." He grinned broadly at Paul. "Look. We're here, all packed and hiking. We're going with you. If we thought you were crazy, we wouldn't be here."

"Right," Amy said. "But before I left the house, I found out something about Charlotte."

"What's that?" Joe asked.

"I turned on the TV while I packed. The news said Charlotte has an invisible dome over it. No one can get in. No one can get out. No communication with anyone inside the dome. Best I can figure, our parents got to Charlotte before the dome appeared."

They all stopped.

"Gabriel said the Adversary was responsible for getting our parents to Charlotte," Paul said. "He said time was short and the Adversary was moving. I didn't understand it all, but I got the feeling we needed to hurry."

"Then, let's." Joe said and started walking, but Paul grabbed his arm and stopped him.

"I have a mission," Paul said as he and Amy joined Joe. "I'm supposed to go to Choteau, Montana. Somewhere there, I'm supposed to find something or do something that will restore the world. Gabriel didn't share any more than that. It's more than two thousand miles. At this point, I would understand if you guys drop out."

"In for a penny, in for a pound," Joe said. "My grandma said that all the time. I couldn't let my best friend deal with this alone."

"I'm not bailing," Amy said. "I couldn't let you two run off like this without me. You'd never make it."

Paul and Joe laughed, but Paul's laugh turned into a groan.

"This whole thing sounds so whacked. Maybe I'm just insane."

"If you are, then we're all insane together." Joe patted Paul on the back.

They started walking again.

"So what's our insane plan?" Amy asked.

"I figure our best shot is to get on Interstate 40," Paul said. "We can hitch rides on that freeway clear through Tennessee."

"Is that safe?" Amy said. "Getting into cars with strangers?"

"Gabriel said God would provide. We have to have faith. If any of us don't want to take a ride with someone," Paul said, "we won't. And there are three of us, so . . . safety in numbers, I guess?"

"There are restaurants and hotels and things near the interchange. That would be a good place to start," Joe said.

"That's what I was thinking," Paul said. "And I need a map."

"We have our tablets," Amy said. "Why . . . " She paused.

"Because we won't always have wireless access," Paul said. "Backup."

#

Paul flipped through the maps at the gas station. There was an Eastern U.S. map providing information about as far as the Mississippi River. He pulled that out and went over to the cashier. Amy and Joe were waiting. They had a Raleigh newspaper and some snack food to add to their inventory. The cashier barely paid attention to them or the transaction. He just took the money and rang up the sale with mechanical motions. Paul swept up the change and they left.

"Did that cashier look a little, um, odd?" Paul asked as they walked toward the on ramp for I-40 West.

"Yes," Amy said. "Joe tried a joke on him and got nothing."

Joe shrugged. "Some folks have no sense of humor."

They found a wide spot on the side of the ramp and started hitchhiking. Paul stood with his thumb out while Joe and Amy read the newspaper stories out loud. There was a story about Charlotte and the dome, more about the white and black fogs, and some new reports from other cities in the U.S. The citizens of one city had woken to a plague of locusts. Another had an outbreak of killer clowns.

As the sun sank near the horizon, it started getting hard to read.

"I hope we get a ride before dark!" Amy said.

"Someone should stop soon," Paul assured her. On the way up the ramp, they hadn't seen any No Hitchhiking signs. He didn't feel so confident himself, though. Cars coming up the ramp now had headlights on.

Then an older model pickup pulled over just past them. Paul ran up to the passenger door.

"You heading west?" he asked the driver, a man of about twenty.

"Yeah. I'm going as far as Statesville," he said. He had shoulder-length brown hair and a friendly smile. "It's a good exit. I know how important that is when you're hitching. It won't be fast, but we'll get there."

"Great."

"I only have room for one up front. The others will have to sit in the bed."

Paul waved the others up.

"Who wants to ride up front?" he asked. "I know we aren't supposed to, but I'm not worried about riding in back. It's getting dark, so no one will see us. Besides, God will provide, right?"

"I'll ride in back," Amy said. "Joe can take the front seat."

"Okay, pile in."

Backpacks went into the pickup bed, with Paul and Amy; Joe climbed into the cab. Paul and Amy hunkered down in the back as the driver ground the shifter into first gear and rolled onto the freeway.

Amy and Paul sat up against the cab in back and pulled coats out of their packs to wrap around themselves. It was cool and windy, but not uncomfortable. They chatted for a while, then Amy nodded off, her head on his shoulder. He could see Joe through the back window, chatting with the driver. Paul sat thinking and praying, and watching the headlights and taillights of the cars on the interstate.

On one hand, he felt excited to begin the journey. On the other, he felt afraid, alone, and unsure. Gabriel had said God would provide, and they'd made a start. He prayed that God would continue to provide and grant him the wisdom and strength to keep going.

CHAPTER SIX

Fog

THE PICKUP driver was kind enough to drop them near the McDonald's in Statesville, and not at the crossroads junction of I-77 and I-40. Here they could take advantage of the facilities at the restaurant, then get on the busier westbound ramp from US 21 to I-40.

Paul located a booth in McDonald's with a power outlet. They got some food, settled down with their tablets, and connected to the free wireless. They searched for news reports and got an idea of what might lie ahead.

"Chicago is having floods from Lake Michigan. The water is just rising up into the city and then flushing back out," Joe said, reading a report on the screen.

"Good thing we aren't planning to go that direction," Amy said, she shivered. "Hmm. Yeah, let's avoid Chicago."

"I think avoiding all the major metros will be good," Paul said. "There'll be challenges just about anywhere, but the big cities have roving gangs on top of everything else. Things are breaking down."

Paul looked around the restaurant, a typical McDonald's. Not a lot of people were around this time of evening. The staff seemed in a half-trance, but not threatening or dangerous. Otherwise, no one seemed to be paying any attention to the three travelers.

"I'm starting to worry, though," Paul said. "Have you noticed that people, like the people behind the counter here, seem, uh, disconnected?"

"Yeah, I noticed that when we stopped before," Joe said. "The pickup driver was nice enough, though."

"Yeah, I saw you talking his ear off," Paul said. "But some of the other people . . . "

"I think," Amy said as she looked around the restaurant, "we should always be prepared to run at a moment's notice. How are your tablet batteries right now?"

"Mine's full," Joe said.

"Mine, too," said Paul.

"Then unplug and pack away the cords. It's easy to slip the tablets back in the bags and run. Let's finish eating, make restroom visits, and get out on the ramp."

It was a bit of a hike from the McDonald's down the Turnersburg Highway to the ramp to I-40, but the area was well lit. Paul put his thumb out, while Amy and Joe stood nearby.

"Think they can see you coming along there?" Joe asked, shielding his eyes from the headlight glare.

"Yeah, we're visible enough," Paul said. "Too bad we can't just walk along the freeway."

"That's where we would get picked up by a cop," Amy said. "If we didn't get killed first by a truck or something."

It was a while before anyone stopped. Near midnight, as Joe was taking his turn with his thumb out, a large black sedan pulled over.

"Heading west?" the driver asked when Paul trotted up to the open window on the passenger-side door.

"Yes. Toward Nashville," Paul said. He could see the driver's face, clean-cut, smiling.

"Boy, you are in luck! That's where I'm heading and I could use some company. I have a long night on the road ahead. Climb on in!"

The Lord God provides, Paul thought as he got in front with the driver, who introduced himself as Daniel. "Just so ya know," he said, "I never liked being called 'Dan.'" Paul thought Daniel seemed about the same age as his father.

"Where you from?" Daniel asked as they sped up the ramp and merged onto the interstate. "You're pretty young to be out here on the road, especially this time of night." He paused, frowned, then said, "Especially with the things happening now."

"We live near Raleigh," Paul said, not wanting to give away too much.

"You're not heading to Music City to join a country band, are you?" Daniel said, then gave a hearty laugh.

"No," Paul said with a chuckle. "No, we're just trying to figure out what's going on."

It wasn't much of an answer, but Daniel accepted it. He nodded and his smile faded. "Yeah, pretty weird, eh? I'm from Wilmington. I'm in the music business and have meetings in Nashville, but when I heard about the weirdness in Charlotte today, I skirted around it. I just hope I can reach Nashville before anything bad happens there. Seems like no matter what's happening in the world, life and work just go on."

Paul introduced Amy and Joe and mentioned that all their parents were stuck in Charlotte.

Daniel gave Paul a couple quick takes. "What are you, fifteen? Sixteen?"

"Fourteen," Joe said. Paul wasn't entirely certain he should have admitted that.

"Bummer," Daniel said. "I don't suppose any of you can drive, either?"

"No," Amy said. "But we'll do our best to help you stay awake."

"I appreciate that," he said. He held up his travel mug. "I'm well caffeinated. Like I said, it's gonna be a long night on the road."

Paul and Amy continued to chat with Daniel. Joe took a nap. The night sped by as they rolled down the road.

#

About an hour later Daniel slowed and pulled off into a rest stop.

"This is a blessing," he said. "Just when needed." He parked close to the restrooms. "Get out and stretch. I'll be back in a few."

After taking advantage of the facilities at the rest stop, Paul got the map from his pack. He yawned, stretched, and rubbed his eyes, trying to shake off the fatigue.

He spread the map out on the hood of the car under a light and marked their current location. On the map, it didn't look like they had gone very far. Just a few hours from Raleigh, and still days of travel ahead. He did a quick check of his funds. He hadn't spent much yet. Amy and Joe had some money, but the total of their funds seemed woefully inadequate. He hadn't even considered where they might stay, sleep, shower. Doubts crept into his mind, fear, uncertainty. He wanted to go home, shower, sleep in his own bed, eat breakfast in the kitchen with Roger Rabbit and Sarah. He sighed.

He folded up the map and stuffed it back in the backpack. "Doesn't seem like we're getting far."

"I'm tired," Amy said around a yawn. "I brushed my teeth in the restroom, but I want a shower and my bed."

"I can rough it," Joe said, then added more quietly, "I'd rather not, though."

"Stay close to the car," Paul said. "I have to walk around a little."

"Don't worry, I'll make sure Daniel doesn't leave without us," Amy said.

Paul walked around the picnic area. He needed to stretch his legs, get his blood pumping. He was tempted to run, but resisted. Then something caught his eye, off by the trees. A grayish tan flash. There stood the coyote.

"Yeah, I know who you are, now," he said softly.

"You think you do," came a voice in his head, its tones smooth and slick. Paul stumbled in surprise, but didn't fall. He hadn't expected the thing to talk back.

"You must be getting tired, Paul," the voice continued. "You should just stop and take a break. Hey, maybe you can get across the freeway and pick up a ride home from there."

"How . . . " Paul started.

"I know the way across," the voice continued. "Gather Amy and Joe, you can follow me. You'll be home in no time. Safe and sound."

"I can't. I have a mission." Paul felt frustration and discomfort. He was tired and wanted nothing more than to just curl up and sleep.

"Are you certain?" The coyote sat on his haunches and his tongue lolled out of his open mouth. "What? Did you dream of an angel coming to you with a message? You don't really believe you are on a mission from God, do you?"

Paul quickly reviewed the events of the last couple days. Could all that have been a dream? No, he told himself. Amy and Joe were with him. All their parents were trapped in Charlotte. It couldn't have been a dream.

"Gabriel told me God wants me to do this," he said. "It wasn't a dream."

"Are you are sure about that, Paul?" the voice said. "You are so young, so inexperienced. It's too far. You'll never be able to make the trip. You don't have the funds or other resources. So many bad things are happening in the world, you probably won't survive. You really should just go home."

"I--" Paul started, then rubbed his face with his hands. "I can't just go home. I have to complete the mission. Our parents are in Charlotte. They can't get out unless I do this task."

"You are being badly treated, Paul. Made to go so far for so little. There is no way you can succeed. You're too young, too vulnerable, too inexperienced. Guaranteed to fail. Why don't you just go home?" Something in the tone of the voice changed, suggesting a stench like a sewer. Paul had never known a voice to have a scent before, but this one did.

"What makes you so sure I'm going to fail?" Paul really didn't want to ask, but somehow the question just popped out.

"Oh, that's right--He *chose* you!" the voice in his head laughed a deep, booming laugh, and it seemed to leave a trail of slime behind. "A mere child! To accomplish an impossible mission! Go home, child. You are not Moses, and you never will be. Go home to your bed, your shower. You cannot possibly succeed. I'm sorry, though, you won't go home to your mom or dad, or Roger or Sarah."

"No, I won't go home," Paul said, determination rising through the fog of fatigue. He tried to show resolve he wasn't completely sure he could back up. "What about my mom and dad, Roger and Sarah?"

"Oh, they are in Charlotte. I have them. When this is all done, they will be mine."

"Yours?" Realization suddenly hit Paul. He really stood before the Adversary. Satan. Lucifer.

"Yes, mine. Mine for eternity."

"That can't be possible," Paul said. "They would never go with you."

"Oh, they already answered my call and went to Charlotte. And now I have them."

"You deceived them? You called them to Charlotte?"

"Of course. There is no hope, Paul. None at all. You will fail. The world will be mine. Go home. Give up. Surrender."

"No way!" Paul said, this time louder and with anger building inside him. His breast burned with determination and he fought against the creepy, slimy, smelly ooze pushing its way inside his head.

The coyote's eyes burned bright red. Then it stood, loped off into the trees, and disappeared. Paul shook himself.

"Paul, who are you talking to?" Joe said, running up to him, "We've been calling for you! What are you doing?"

"I saw the coyote again," he said. "This time he spoke to me."

Joe scanned the trees, but the coyote was gone.

"Darn," he said. "I wanted to see him."

"No, Joe, you don't. He's evil."

They returned to the car, and Paul related what the coyote had said. Even Daniel listened.

"If it wasn't for all the stuff going on," Daniel said, "I'd call that a pretty good yarn. Now, though," he looked at them gravely, "I believe you."

"Well, there's more to tell, then," Paul said. He looked back to the trees where the coyote had appeared. "But let's get going first. I don't want to stay around here, especially after seeing him."

As they drove toward Asheville, Paul told the whole story so far. Joe and Amy added their parts when necessary. Every once in a while, Daniel would whistle or make an exclamation.

"That's quite the tale," he said when they ran out of story. "So this Gabriel is probably an angel, eh?"

"I'm pretty sure he is," Paul said. "I don't have any prior experience with them, though."

"And Gabriel seems to think the coyote is the Adversary, the Devil, Satan, Lucifer, whatever?" Daniel took a sip of coffee.

"That's right." Paul felt a tightening in his chest. "That's the feeling I get."

"So, you guys . . . "

"Are on a mission from God," Joe finished.

Daniel chuckled. "Only you aren't the Blues Brothers."

"Who?" Amy asked.

"Never mind."

The road climbed and wound into the Smoky Mountains as they neared Asheville. Wisps of fog floated across the road in the headlights. Then it grew thicker, and thicker. Soon they slowed and

Daniel hugged the white fog stripe on the right side of the lane to keep the car on the road. They just crept along, then.

"Well, I've been through these mountains when they get fogged up," he said. "This is the worst I've ever seen it."

"Do your best, Daniel," Paul said. "Please, don't stop if you can help it."

"I don't plan to," Daniel said.

CHAPTER SEVEN

Zombies

ASHEVILLE GAVE off a fuzzy glow as they approached. Daniel kept the speed down. No other cars were on the road with them, and from what they could see from the freeway, none seemed to be moving on the city roads.

"I know it's hard," Paul said, "but can you keep going?" Something about the fog and the still quiet in Asheville bothered him.

"Yeah, I'd like to. There's an interchange on the other side of town. Hardee's, Shoney's, Cracker Barrel, McDonald's, all that. I need to get gas. Lots of light there. Should be safe to get off. But at this rate, it will be a bit."

Daniel was white-knuckling the wheel. He pried off each hand in turn and shook it to loosen the muscles.

Amy and Joe kept a watch for signs while Paul kept up a calming chatter with Daniel. Part of the chatter involved asking Daniel about his religious background. Yes, Daniel had grown up in a Christian church. No, he hadn't been active in a very long time. Yes, he believed in God and knew about Jesus and the sacrifice.

"So do you have a relationship with Jesus?" Paul asked.

"Well, not in so many words," Daniel said. "But ever since I heard your stories and we hit this fog, I've been praying very hard to get us through this."

"Seriously?"

"Seriously," Daniel said. "I'm feeling a deep need to get back in touch with God. Thanks for helping."

Up ahead, Paul saw the blurred outlines of the Hardee's sign and the McDonald's arches on the other side of the freeway.

"Looks like we're at the interchange you mentioned, Daniel," Joe said.

"Yes," Paul said, pointing ahead. "There's the ramp just up there."

Daniel navigated the tight loop of the ramp and came to a stop at the intersection. It all looked other-worldly and dim. He drove across to the nearest self-serve gas station and filled his tank.

"I need coffee. I vote for McDonald's. What do you say?" he said when he got back into the car.

They all agreed. Daniel turned out of the gas station and they crept through the fog and down the street to the glowing yellow arches.

#

The parking lot was empty, as was the dining room inside. Paul looked at the Shoney's restaurant next door. It was dark and empty. Inside the McDonald's, a young man stood at the counter to take their order. He seemed pale and his movements mechanical. Someone in the kitchen area produced their burgers and set them on the warmer. The young man put the food on a tray and set it on the counter. They took their food and drinks to a large table in the corner with a power outlet.

"Have you noticed how some people are?" Paul asked Daniel. "Zoned out, mechanical."

Daniel looked at the folks behind the counter. "Yeah. That's one reason I picked you guys up. You seemed so . . . normal. Plus I had this feeling it was what I was supposed to do."

Paul looked at Daniel and wondered if God's hand had touched him back in Statesville.

While they ate, they broke out the tablets and checked news and blog sites. A few blogs were speculating on what the root cause of the events were. All seemed very far off target, from Paul's view. No new events in the mainstream press tonight. Was the Adversary taking a breather? He doubted it.

"Not seeing anything new or different," he said, and packed away his tablet and power cord. Amy and Joe did the same. "Mostly reports of looting, fires, gang activity, and disorder in the larger cities."

"The coyote seemed pretty threatening this last time, from what you said, Paul," Amy said. "Especially about our parents. It's almost like he's holding them hostage."

"I'm not sure how to take it yet," Paul said.

"I think he's hoping you'll give up," Joe said. "It's part of the intimidation."

"It's a little different this time," Paul said. "The first couple of times, I was left with this feeling of dread. Gabriel cast that out. I think he protected me, somehow. Still, the coyote made me feel helpless, like I'm not capable. But I have to keep trying."

They started gathering up the trash and Daniel went to get his coffee refilled. When he came back, he had a worried look on his face.

"Don't look around," he said. "Just listen. I've been watching while we ate. There has not been another car along this road since we came in. When we aren't at the counter, Mr. Roboto up there just stands and does nothing. The cook in back doesn't move around, either, when he's not filling an order. Let's get the heck out of here. I'm getting creeped out."

They quickly cleared up and went outside to the car.

"Hey, something moving over there in the fog," Daniel said, pointing toward the Shoney's. "Looks like people."

Paul looked and saw the shifting shadows. "I think we should just get in the car," he said, climbing in the passenger front seat. Amy and Joe were already in the back seat. "Daniel! There are some more down on the street."

Daniel was already in and starting up the sedan. He got the car moving before the doors all slammed shut. He pulled out of the parking spot and his lights hit one of the groups of shadowy shapes. They became clearer, but stranger. They looked like people, but not whole. Many seemed bent at odd angles. They shambled along. One of the people pressed up against the window on Amy's side. She screamed.

Zombies!

Daniel swerved the car around, knocking the group down like bowling pins, and drove toward the group from the Shoney's next door. Zombie pieces and fluids smeared his car and the windows. He swerved again, causing a similar cascade of bodies from the Shoney's group. He worked the windshield washer and wipers as he drove toward the street outlet to the Smoky Park Highway, then turned left toward the interstate. More of the shambling zombies were scattered around the highway.

"Don't hit any more head-on," Joe said. "They smear up your windshield!"

Daniel navigated between as best he could, avoiding hitting any head-on. The fog wasn't as thick, now, so identifying the westbound ramp wasn't difficult. He swung the sedan onto the ramp, taking out another small group of shamblers, and gunned the engine.

"Gonna have to wash the car," he said, knuckles white on the wheel and sweat beading on his forehead.

"Old-school zombies," Joe said. "Slow."

"That's a good thing," Paul said. "I just hope we don't run into the fast ones somewhere."

"Don't jinx it, Paul," Joe looked out the back window. "Those may be next."

Paul turned in his seat to look at Amy. She was white as a sheet, but collecting herself and trying not to look at the zombie smear on the window.

"The coyote did this," she said, voice a little shaky. "Didn't he?"

"Yeah, I'm thinking that," Paul said. "The troll, the zombies. He's throwing these things in our path. Finding our fear."

"Fear, yeah," Joe said. "Get us so afraid we turn back. If we turn back, he wins."

Daniel mumbled something as he drove.

"Are you okay, Daniel?" Paul asked.

"Yeah," he said. "Just praying. I'm finding strength there."

"Good," Paul said. "We need you."

"Well, I could blame you guys for all this. But when I thought and prayed about it, I realized if I hadn't picked you up I might have been here alone. I have a feeling your coyote, the Adversary, isn't concerned about collateral damage. Where did those zombies come from? The local cemetery, or the residents of Asheville?"

The other three were quiet, taking that in.

"Yeah," Daniel said, answering his own question. "The Adversary is evil, all right. Those zombies were probably citizens just a day ago. This is serious. You kids need to succeed, make it right."

They drove on through the night leaving the fog and zombies behind in Asheville.

#

A couple of hours later, they pulled off the freeway at a truck stop near Knoxville, Tennessee.

"I'm going to gas up again, and wash the zombie stuff off the car," Daniel said, "and I need to get out and stretch. The sun is about to come up, and there is a lot of activity around here. Folks look normal."

He pointed to people coming to and going from the station and working the gas pumps.

"You suppose the zombie-ness was isolated to North Carolina?" Joe said.

"Maybe, or maybe just more remote areas," Daniel said. He looked around the store. "This is a truck stop. You'll find them all across the country and you should look for them."

"But we're not truckers," Paul said.

"No, but I bet the rules are being bent now," Daniel said. "They have showers and facilities that are usually for professional truckers. But you can sometimes talk the staff into letting you in. They don't look too busy now. Try it while I gas up and wash the car."

"One can only try," Paul said and led Joe and Amy to the cashier. No, they weren't professional drivers, Paul told the woman behind the counter, but they really needed showers. Couldn't she make an exception for some poor, tired kids? The cashier smiled and gave in. Paul thought it was worth the few dollars. They took shifts, with one watching packs and the entrances while the others showered and changed.

"I'm not all that hungry," Joe said when they gathered up the packs, "but I could use a hot cocoa."

"I want coffee," Amy said.

They found a table in the cafe section with power and ordered coffee and cocoa, and Paul was working on a slice of apple pie when Daniel found them.

"I've been on the phone with my associates in Nashville," he said. "We're just a couple hours away. Ah, took advantage of the showers, I see." He looked them over. "Good. Truck stops are a blessing.

Anyway, I can't go any further with you after Nashville. I don't know anyone going toward Montana, but you might be able to make a connection there. You don't want to go toward Oklahoma. They said Oklahoma City is being hit with huge sand storms, with sand dune drifts covering half the city. I think you need to head north. I can swing around via Old Hickory Boulevard in Nashville and get you to I-24."

Paul got out the map and they looked at the possible routes from Nashville.

"That will take us toward St. Louis. From there we can head toward Iowa and west," Paul said.

"That makes sense," Joe said. "Of course, I've never been through this part of the country, so my opinion is worth about as much as this cup of cocoa. Maybe less."

"Too many routes north will lead to Chicago," Amy said. "We want to avoid that, so whenever we can, we should choose a westward route."

And suddenly, Gabriel was sitting at their table.

"Amy has some good advice. Avoid Chicago. Also, avoid getting into any major metropolitan areas," he said.

Paul look at Gabriel and smiled. He felt relieved when the angel appeared; his uncertainty seemed to just fade away. Daniel looked at Gabriel open-mouthed.

"And thank you, Daniel, for your steadfast and earnest support of these young people."

Tears came to Daniel's eyes. "I wasn't certain," he said. "Now I am. You're Gabriel?"

"Yes."

"What is going on?" Daniel asked.

"The Adversary is breaking some rules. Paul has been chosen to restore the world."

"Rules?" Amy asked.

"You know the rules, Amy," Gabriel said. "You know your Bible well. You also know the plan of salvation. This is all bound up in the rules, for lack of a better term. When the Adversary was driven from heaven, rules were set up and God established the road to your salvation. Your souls are the harvest. Now the Adversary has grown impatient with the rules and caused chaos. Paul is chosen to restore order and the rules. He accepted the mission."

"Are you, like, a guardian angel?" Daniel asked.

"No," Gabriel said. "I am just the messenger."

"Oh," Daniel said.

"One message was of thanks to you, Daniel. Another is to be careful and watchful. Dangers are placed in your path by the Adversary." He looked at each of them in turn. "Daniel's assessment isn't quite correct. The Adversary isn't just indifferent to collateral damage. He thrives on it. The more destruction, loss of life, and damnation of souls he can cause, the more he likes it. He is nothing like your crime lords or supervillains from your fiction stories. He is the enemy. The one enemy. He is the Deceiver. Be ever mindful."

"Thank you, Gabriel," Paul said.

The angel laid his hand on Paul's shoulder. "Thank you, Paul, for taking this burden. Just remember, the Lord God will provide."

Gabriel stood and left.

CHAPTER EIGHT

Stopped

THEY RODE through the breaking morning in the central Tennessee countryside. Joe and Amy dozed in the back seat; Paul kept watch on Daniel and the road from the front. As they took the exit near Nashville onto Old Hickory, Paul observed the activity around the city. Cars moved about in the early morning and he could see people going about their business. *I wonder if the Adversary just isn't bothering with Nashville,* he thought.

He asked Daniel about his business and the music industry.

"It's a tough business," Daniel said. "Like anything that makes an obscene amount of money, there are a lot of bad people involved. But there are good people, too. Those people depend on me. I try to keep the honest people honest and the bad people from taking too much."

Old Hickory wasn't the fastest road, but kept them from the core of Nashville. Smoke rose from a few fires on the east side of the city. Paul could see the ramp to I-24 was just down the road when Daniel pulled into a gas station.

"Well, this is where I can let you off," he said. "I wish I could take you all the way to Montana, but I have commitments here I have to meet. Like Gabriel said, the Lord God will provide."

They got out and said their goodbyes to Daniel. Amy gave him a hug.

"Stay safe, Daniel," she said.

"I will. And I'll pray for you guys. Don't take any side trips and stay focused on the mission."

"We will," Paul said. "Thanks for everything."

Daniel got back in his sedan and drove off.

#

Traffic on the northbound ramp at I-24 was light. The three sat on the side of the road for a couple of hours, munching the last of their sandwiches and sipping water.

"Wow, I thought we'd get a ride sooner than this," Joe said after they had eaten. He was taking his turn with his thumb out. At least, he had his thumb out when cars were coming up the ramp. Just then, he had both thumbs in his jeans pockets. "I wish there was a more reliable way to go."

"We could try a train," Amy suggested.

"I don't think trains are as easy to hop as the movies show," Paul said. "That's probably more Hollywood mythology. We'd better not risk it."

"Of course, we have no idea which train is going which direction anyway," Joe said. "We could end up in New York or Florida."

"I wish one of us could drive," Amy said. She wrapped her arms around her legs and rested her chin on her knees. "How about bicycles?"

"Yeah, let's see," Paul said opening the map. "We have more than eighteen hundred miles left to go. I don't think I'm up for trying to do that on a bicycle."

"We still have eighteen hundred miles?" Joe said.

"Yep," Paul said. "Still, we've gone more than five hundred miles just on our good looks."

Amy laughed. Joe looked disgusted.

"I thought it was only two thousand miles total!" Joe said.

"It's about twenty-three hundred, depending on the routes we take," Paul said. "I'm sure we won't be going along the most direct route."

Joe frowned. "It just seems to get longer and longer."

"We can't let a couple of hours standing on the side of the road weigh us down," Paul said. "C'mon, Joe, sit down. It's Amy's turn. She'll probably change our luck."

"Luck, luck, luck," Amy said getting up and brushing off her jeans. "I'd prefer some divine intervention."

Just then, an old flat-bed truck with wood sides on the bed pulled up and stopped. Joe ran up to the passenger door.

"You heading toward St. Louis?" Joe asked at the open window.

The driver was an older man wearing a flannel shirt and a beat-up, old straw hat. "Sure," he said, "but I only go as far as Paducah."

"That works," said Joe.

"There's fresh straw in the back, you guys can settle in there," the man said.

"See?" Paul said as they climbed into the back of the truck. "Amy did change our luck."

When they were settled in, Paul patted the back of the cab. The man smiled back at them through the window, waved, and got the truck rolling.

The straw made the ride pretty comfortable, so they took advantage of the opportunity to catch up on sleep. Paul sat and watched out the back of the truck bed as the countryside passed. The terrain was rolling here, with trees and farms. They also passed by the grounds of Fort Campbell. Soon, Paul dozed off.

He and the others awoke to a bouncing jolt. They were slowing down and turning. Paul twisted around and looked through the window. They left the freeway and were rolling down a ramp.

"We must be at or near Paducah," he said.

They all shook the sleep off and brushed away the straw sticking to their clothing and hair. They gathered their packs and the truck pulled over to the side of the road.

"Sorry about the bump," the man said coming around the back. "I turn off here and head to the farm. Hope you can get a ride from here." He helped them down.

"Well, we got a nice nap, anyway," Joe said shaking the man's hand. "Thanks!"

The man got back into his truck and drove off.

"It seems like we were only riding for a few minutes," Amy said.

"You guys fell asleep," Paul said, not admitting to his own nap. "We needed that, though. Let's get on the other side. There's some traffic here. Let's not waste any time."

They managed to get safely across a busy six-lane road and up the ramp on the other side. Paul stuck his thumb out, and almost immediately, a car pulled over. It was a two-door, but it had plenty of room in the back, so they jumped in.

"St. Louis, eh?" the driver asked as they drove up the ramp. He wore a denim shirt and ball cap and Paul thought he looked about thirty. "Yeah, should be there in about two and a half hours. I have a full tank, so we can just roll."

Joe, who sat in the front this time, asked Paul for the map. "We're going well beyond St. Louis. Where are you going?"

"I was going to Chicago, but things aren't good there." He scratched the stubble on his cheek.

"Yeah, we heard about the floods from the lake," Amy said.

"I'm not sure about St. Louis, either," the driver said. "I'm Jake, by the way, and I'm out looking for work. I'm a lineman."

"What's a lineman?" Amy asked.

"I work on those power poles and high towers," Jake pointed up at the power lines they passed.

Amy introduced everyone. "What do you mean by 'not sure' about St. Louis?"

"Well, I usually can get weather and news about St. Louis on the radio or online," Jake said holding his smartphone up. "But today, nothing."

"Nothing?" Joe asked.

"Nope, nothing," Jake said. "Nothing about weather, crime, events, or anything."

Joe looked at the pair in the back seat. "We haven't seen the coyote today, have we?"

"No," Paul said. "But that doesn't mean he hasn't done something."

"What are you talking about?" Jake asked, changing lanes and passing a tractor-trailer.

"It's kind of a long story," Paul said.

"About all the weird stuff going on?" Jake said. He nodded. "Things just got crazy back in Memphis and I got laid off. I heard there might be some work up north. I left my wife and kids in Memphis until I can find something."

"I hope you find something soon, Jake," Amy said.

Paul related their story to date. Jake listened, and asked questions for more detail, especially about Asheville.

"Zombies in Asheville!" he said. "You're kidding, right?"

"No," Paul said, "And, well, there's an angel, too."

"Really?"

"His name is Gabriel. He's a messenger," Amy said. She told how he appeared in Knoxville and talked to them, then just left.

"Kinda comes and goes, eh?" Jake seemed to be chewing hard on all the information. "So we have the Devil in the form of a coyote, and an angel that comes and goes, and three kids on a mission from God. You met a troll and a pack of zombies. That about the sum of it so far?"

"Yeah," Paul said. "So far."

"That is pretty amazing," Jake said. "Wow!"

Jake drove in silence for a while. Paul worried. Would he reject their story? Throw them out of the car? The longer Jake was silent, the more Paul worried.

Finally, he broke the silence. "You guys are just pretty brave. Pretty brave."

Paul was relieved, and he could see Joe and Amy were too. They started sharing information about what had happened in various places around the world and speculated on what the Adversary was doing.

"Well, I wouldn't spend a lot of time worrying about what he's trying to do," Jake said. "We all know what he wants. The Devil wants to screw up the whole plan of salvation. What I'd try to figure out is what he's going to lay in your path."

"I'm worried about what you said about St. Louis," Paul said. "Let's stop somewhere before we get too close and see if we can find out what's going on there."

"Good idea," Jake said.

About half an hour from St. Louis, Jake pulled off the freeway and they found a McDonald's across the road from a field of corn. At Amy's suggestion, they drove around the store in the car first, then picked a parking spot near the entrance. Jake back into the spot for a quick getaway.

"Are we getting paranoid?" Joe asked.

"No more than is healthy," Paul said.

They got out, and the trio carried their backpacks.

"No offense, Jake," Paul said. "We don't plan on running off."

"None taken," Jake said. "I'd be careful, too, if I were you guys."

"Besides, McD's has free Wi-Fi," Joe said.

Amy went to buy a *St. Louis Post-Dispatch* from a newspaper box near the door, but there were no papers there. Another box for a St. Louis weekly paper was empty, as well.

"Okay, that idea was a bust," she said.

Inside, they encountered the usual mechanical staff, and a few customers who seemed normal.

"Seems like the service staff at these places are just robots," Jake said.

They claimed a table not far from the door and settled down there.

Jake watched them work the tablets. Searches pulled up nothing from St. Louis newer than a couple of days old. No news, sports, or weather, and no crime news. It wasn't looking good. A customer tossed the remains of his meal in the trash nearby and turned to go out the door.

"Sir, can you tell us what's going on in St. Louis?" Joe said directly to the man. He looked like a farmer, dressed in coveralls, flannel shirt, and boots, with weathered face and hands.

He turned and looked at him, blue eyes shining and alive. "No, son, I can't. St. Louis just . . . stopped."

"Stopped?" Joe asked.

"Yes, stopped. That's best I can describe it. No one wants to go there. Some as have, never came back."

"How close can you get?" Paul asked.

"I suspect Fairview Heights is as close as you want to get." He gave them all a solemn look. "If you don't have to go there, I'd find another way around." He turned and left.

Paul dug out the map. He spread it out on the table. Fairview Heights. Yeah, there it was, just before East St. Louis and the convenient beltway around the city.

"Man, that's the only easy crossing of the Mississippi," Jake said.

Paul squinted at the map. The area around St. Louis had blurred and faded.

"Hey, guys, look at this," he said, pointing at the place on the map where St. Louis was supposed to be.

"Uh, oh," Joe said.

Paul looked at Amy, then back at the map. He knew she would

object to what he was going to say, but there wasn't any other way.

"We can get around this, but we'll have to take some back roads," he said, finger on the map. "First, we get on County Road 50, just down here, and go north until we get to Road 143 and head west. There's a town called Edwardsville. We can get more information there. We need to find a good place to cross the Mississippi."

"That's north," Amy said.

"Yeah, but not for long," Paul said. "We can't cross the river here."

Paul looked at Jake.

"Well," Jake said, "there's a bridge we can cross in Louisiana, a little town up the river, and another further north at Hannibal. We can try for Louisiana first."

"That's getting pretty close to Chicago," Amy said.

"We get across there," Paul said, pointing to Louisiana, "then we head for Des Moines and west."

"She's got a bug for Chicago," Joe said, in answer to a quizzical look from Jake. "Gabriel warned us away from there and from metro areas."

"Okay," Amy said. "Make sure we don't go any further north. I get a bad feeling about that."

CHAPTER NINE

Frogs

THEY FOUND their way through to Edwardsville. The roads were just country two-lane blacktops, but they were good roads. Traffic was light and they made reasonable time. They arrived in late afternoon. The weather was changing, with rain clouds building up to the northwest.

"Man, you can smell the rain in the air," Paul said. He waved his hand in the moving air from the open window as they drove through town and turned northwest on Edwardsville Road. "And we're driving right into it."

"That looks like a good old fashioned midwestern thunderstorm brewing," Jake said. "It'll be here in a few minutes."

Jake was right. In a few blocks, large drops of rain smacked the windshield and the wind kicked up. Everyone cranked up windows before the rain came down in earnest. Then a flash of lightning and the crash of thunder announced the full arrival of the storm.

Jake turned the wipers on high as the rain drenched visibility, then strange thuds sounded on the roof and hood of the car.

"What's that?" Jake said, peering through the blurry windshield.

Paul leaned forward and looked as more and more thuds hit the car. Large hailstones? But . . . green, and with legs? One landed with a splat on the windshield and Paul saw the bulging eyes.

"Those are frogs!" Paul said, incredulous. "Frogs!"

Frogs bounced off the car and added to the shiny green layer covering the road, the sidewalks, the yards and the roofs of the apartments and other buildings. The car ran over the slimy green things and Jake slowed and pull over into a vacant lot. Paul heard the frogs squishing and crunching under the car tires. The car slid to a stop in the muddy vacant lot.

It went on raining frogs and water. Lightning flashed and thunder blasted as they sat in the car watching.

"We'll have to wait this out," Jake yelled through the din of the storm. He turned off the engine.

Paul looked out the window. Most of the frogs died after hitting the ground, buildings, or cars, but a few lived. The live frogs crawled and jumped around on the piles of dead ones, and the rainwater made huge puddles around the piles. After a few more minutes, the frogs stopped falling, but the rain continued.

"Hey," Joe said, looking out his side, "the frogs are moving! No, wait. It's the water. The road is turning into a stream."

Everyone looked out the left side windows. Sure enough, the water flowed down the road, carrying most of the frogs with it.

"Well, maybe it'll wash them all away and we can get going soon," Amy said. She sounded hopeful, but the rain kept coming down. If anything, the flow increased, still carrying live and dead frogs.

"I hope it doesn't get much deeper," Jake said. "If it gets up to the doors, we could be in trouble."

They huddled together and watched as the deluge continued. The flood rose, the light faded under the storm clouds, and the frogs floated by. Thunder and lightning added sudden and violent punctuation to the dark, gloomy scene. Eventually, the sound and flash tapered off, the darkness ebbed, and the rain slacked. Outside, the flood started to dwindle.

Fewer frogs were in the flow, and the flood turned from frog-green to a muddy color with green spots. Soon it was just a shallow, muddy wash across the road. Still, frogs covered the yards and buildings.

Jake started the car and pulled out in the road again. The muddy surface was slick, so he had to drive slowly, but they were moving again.

"Okay, now we can add a plague of frogs to what we've encountered," Paul said. "Boy, is that going to be a mess to clean up."

Amy looked out the back window. "That was just gross," she said. She shivered and turned around.

The road improved as they drove north--still wet from the drenching rain, but clear. The sun broke out in places and dappled the countryside with sunny spots. Jake opened his window and let some freshly rain-scrubbed air into the stuffy car.

"Ah! That feels good!" he said.

"And there's the rainbow," Paul said, pointing back to the right where a rainbow arched over a cornfield.

"Yes, a rainbow! God's promise," Amy shifted in her seat to get a better view. "As bad as it may get, we can be sure the world won't be destroyed by water again." She looked down, thinking. "I wonder if he used the rain to wash away the frogs? Kind of beating the Adversary at his own game?"

They continued through Jerseyville and Carrollton, then turned west. The road cut through alternating farmland and hill country, crossed the Illinois River and some more forested hills, then wound down into the Mississippi River proper.

"There's the Mississippi River," Joe said.

Jake nodded. "It's pretty big, here, but not as wide as farther south. There are places it's about a mile or so wide."

"That's the largest river we've seen yet," Paul said.

They followed the river north and Paul could see barges tied up along the bank. Then the road turned away and swung through a couple of small towns. Finally, they turned west.

"What's that barge doing?" Paul asked, pointing north of the bridge. A barge, heavily laden with cargo containers, was moving south with the current. It was sideways and near the east bank. "Is it going to hit the bridge?"

"I'm not waiting to find out," Jake said. He gunned the engine and the car sped across the bridge on the US 54 Expressway. Behind them, they saw the barge slam into one of the bridge supports. On the other side of the river, the bridge started to collapse.

"We're across," Amy said.

"That was close," Joe said.

"I suppose that was the Adversary's work," Paul said. *But,* he asked himself, *how did he know we would come this way?*

They drove through Louisiana and turned north again, heading toward Des Moines, Iowa.

"So what is Des Moines?" Amy asked.

"A city," Paul said.

"No, I mean the words. Are they French?"

"Oh, yeah, I guess it is French," Paul said. "Yeah, I wonder what that means."

"I used to know that," Jake said. "Just can't remember."

"We can check next time we stop, if there's wireless," Amy said.

It was full dark by the time they reached the next stop, Mt. Pleasant. The usual roadside services weren't there, but they did find Jerry's Restaurant. The establishment claimed presidents had dined there.

"No Wi-Fi," Amy said, looking at her tablet screen.

"No big deal," Joe said.

"I'm not sure," Amy said. "I get a feeling we need to know this."

"Know what?" Joe asked blankly.

"The meaning of Des Moines! Remember? We were just talking about it."

"Well, I'll check," Joe said and went up to the cashier, an older woman. She didn't know but she thought someone else would. She went into an office in the back. When she returned, she had an answer.

"For what it's worth," Joe said, sitting down, "Des Moines is French for monks, or The Monks. Something like that."

"Monks?" Paul said.

"Monks," Amy said. "That's significant. I just don't know how."

"I remember something about that," Jake said. "The name may not actually be all French, but some mashup from the old French trappers and Native American. I could be wrong."

"Amy has a feeling about it," Paul said. "That tells me we may encounter something there."

"The way I'm feeling about it," she said, "means something bad."

"And a city that 'stopped' or a plague of frogs isn't bad, eh?" Joe said.

"From here, we're mostly going west," Paul said. "Do your feelings have anything to do with how close we are to Chicago?"

Amy thought. "No. I mean, I have a bad feeling about Chicago, but it's a different bad feeling. I'm sorry. I know that doesn't make sense."

"Well, we have a couple of hours to Des Moines," Jake said. "It'll be a little late when we get there. I'll be getting a motel. What do you guys want to do?"

Paul thought about how much money he had left. His little stash was slowly dwindling. Another truck stop would be perfect, budget-wise.

"How much do you guys have left?" Paul asked Joe and Amy.

"Not enough for a motel," Joe said.

"Me either," Amy said. "I suppose there's a truck stop where we can clean up, at least?"

"Yeah, I think there's a Pilot on the other side of Des Moines," Jake said. "There are a few motels nearby. I can drop you guys at the truck stop."

"Sounds like a plan," Paul said.

But it didn't sound good at all. It sounded awful. Paul's eyes were hot and gritty from lack of sleep, and he ached all over. He longed for a home-cooked meal and a long sleep in his own bed. Truck stops were okay, and he knew he should be grateful for the opportunity to take a shower, but what he really wanted was home. And what was the deal with Amy's "feeling" about Des Moines or monks or whatever it was? He wanted this whole crazy mess to be over, but it wasn't, not by a long shot.

CHAPTER TEN

Monks

DES MOINES glowed in the night as they approached. Paul, Amy, and Joe had slept off and on most of the way from Mt. Pleasant. Jake took the I-235 freeway to the west side of the city and found the truck stop.

"Look, I have to find work, and I heard there are companies here who need linemen," Jake said. "I have a wife and kids, I can't go any further with you. I'll pray for you. I hope you succeed."

"You've been great, Jake," Paul said. "We appreciate all you've done."

"Yes, you've been great," Amy said and gave Jake a hug.

Joe shook Jake's hand and thanked him. "Be careful," Jake said.

Jake drove off. Paul, Amy, and Joe entered the truck stop and made arrangements for showers. They had this routine down, so they were showered, changed and ready to travel again in a half-hour.

"Yeah, we should do some laundry soon," Joe said. "I think I have one clean change left."

"Me, too," Paul said. "They have machines here. This may be our best chance."

"If we combine the clothing, we can get it done in one load," Amy said. "We should be finished in less than two hours. Of course, I'm not all excited about washing my clothes with yours."

"Picky," Joe said.

Paul looked out at the freeway and thought a moment.

"We have time," he said. "Let's do it."

Amy organized the laundry. While waiting for the clothes to dry,

Paul found a piece of white poster board, and--with a borrowed black marker--wrote the word "WEST" on it in large block letters. After packing their clean clothes away, they hiked down to Douglas Parkway. Not far was the ramp to I-80.

"We need a sign?" Joe asked

"Yeah, a couple miles from here, the freeway splits," Paul said. "We want to make sure we get a ride on the right freeway."

"Monks," Amy said and pointed.

Under the lights of the intersection about 50 meters down the same side of the parkway, three people stood on the side of the road. They wore long, brown, hooded robes. Three more, also dressed in robes, walked toward them from the far side of the truck stop.

A chill ran down Paul's spine. This was not okay.

"We need to cross the street," Paul said, looking up and down the parkway. They weren't at an intersection, but that didn't seem important right now. "We're clear, let's go!"

They ran across one set of lanes, then stumbled down and up the ditch median and across the other lanes. When Paul looked back from the other side of the parkway, all six monks stood on the roadside under the light. The monks seemed to be watching them.

"Let's get to the ramp," Paul said.

They ran down the side of the parkway, stumbling in the dark, helping each other on the uneven footing.

They were a little way up the ramp when Paul stopped to look back. The monks just stood in a line under the light at the intersection. Still watching.

"That's just weird," Joe said.

"Yeah," Paul said. "Let's keep going up the ramp a ways, but not completely out of the light from the intersection."

Paul stopped a short way up the ramp, turned and held up the sign and his thumb. Joe kept an eye on the monks in case they started moving their way. Amy guarded the packs.

No one stopped. A lot of cars and trucks rolled by without so much as a tap on the brakes. Joe paced near the packs.

"I think we need some prayer, Amy," Paul said after a string of vehicles went past, ignoring them.

"I'm up for it. Let's hold hands."

They made a small circle and prayed. Paul prayed, particularly, to keep the monks away and to keep them safe. Amy prayed for a safe ride. Joe prayed for a long ride, but kept checking on the monks down the road. At the "Amen," Paul checked the monks, too. Six more had arrived at the intersection and joined the first group on the other side of the parkway.

Another group of six monks was coming up the ramp.

"Grab your gear," Paul said. "We have to run." He slung his pack over his shoulder and turned up the ramp, only to see more monks coming from the freeway.

"This isn't good," Joe said.

A car sped up the ramp from the intersection. It stopped with screeching tires and doors opening.

"Get in," a woman's voice yelled. "Get in, now!"

They barely made it into the car and got the doors closed before the woman driver gunned the engine and sped out to the freeway.

Another woman sat in the passenger seat. She was a small, middle-aged woman with short, curly hair. "We saw you praying while we sat at the light," she said. "I'm Emily, and this is Sally. You looked so precious, and we saw the monks watching you, so we knew we had to pick you up."

Sally, the driver, looked taller and more serious. She had long, straight, graying hair

Emily looked at the sign Paul held. "I'm sorry, we're going south. But we can take you to the exit that puts you right on 80. It's just two exits down."

"We've been dealing with the monks for a couple of days now," Sally said, speaking for the first time since picking them up. "They move in groups of three and they can turn people, somehow. But it seems they have to have six to turn one person."

"What do you mean 'turn?'" Amy asked.

"Turn you into a monk like them," Emily said. "They've been spreading and turning people for the last couple of days. There are a lot of them now. Most of the city is lost to them."

"How do you keep from getting caught and turned by them?" Joe asked.

"They don't move fast and if you're never alone, it takes more of them," Sally said. "You have to be ready to fight them off if they do start coming. It doesn't take a lot to put one down. That's about all we've figured out about them. We don't know much else."

"How do you fight them?" Amy asked.

"Sticks, rocks, whatever you can get your hands on," Emily said. "Don't let them touch you and especially don't let them surround you. Get six surrounding you and you get turned."

Emily explained that she and Sally had both lost their husbands to the monks the first day they showed up. Once in the hooded robes, the husbands were anonymous and under some other control. Her voice cracked and shook as she described what happened. She and Sally had decided to go south to stay with relatives.

"We wouldn't have picked you up," Sally said, her voice tense. "But you were praying and we knew we just couldn't leave you to those things."

"You guys looked so precious, we just had to stop," Emily said again, dabbing at a tear.

Paul thought back to the zombies and wondered if the changes were permanent. *Will this reverse when I complete the mission?* he thought. *Will these poor people be restored?*

And with that, the ride was over. Sally pulled over a bit before the off ramp and let them out. She got out, too, and opened the trunk.

"I have extra staffs, you should each take one," Sally said, pulling three wooden staffs from the trunk. "We broke into a martial arts store and grabbed a bunch of these. They're called bōs and they work great against the monks. My advice, attack before they get enough numbers to turn you. They aren't much for fighters. When they get close, you'll feel the fear. That's what they depend on, fear. Knock a threesome down and they all go up in a puff of smoke."

The bōs were about six feet long and slightly tapered from the middle out.

"They also make good walking sticks," Sally said.

"Thanks!" Amy smiled as she hefted one and got a feel for it. "This will be great!"

"Yeah," Paul looked at the bō he held. "Thanks! We'll keep that in mind."

"I-80 is just down there," Sally said, pointing to the ramp. "Stay together and be tough. We'll be praying for you!"

She got back in her car and drove off. Paul could briefly see Emily waving through the back window, and he waved back.

At least this ramp had lights, so they weren't completely in the dark. It's getting late, Paul thought as they hiked up the ramp. He set them up under a lamp for visibility.

"How do you feel about attacking the monks?" Joe asked.

"I'm a little uncomfortable with that," Paul said. "But I think if we saw more . . . well, we'd have to see."

"After what Sally and Emily said," Amy said, "I'm all for attacking. I'm creeped out now."

"I don't know anything about using a staff as a weapon, Amy," Paul said.

"It's okay," she spun her bō. "The bō is my favorite weapon in martial arts. I'll show you a few things. If what they said is true, we should be able to fight them with just a couple of simple techniques."

She showed them how to hold the staffs, and ways to strike the head and center of body. She made them practice the moves. Then she showed off a bit, spinning and whipping the bō around. *She'll be dangerous if the monks showed up,* Paul thought.

No cars passed for a while, and Joe took up the sign. Then he froze, looking down the ramp back the way they had walked up. Paul followed his gaze. Three monks were standing under a light down there, looking toward them.

"They're behind us, too!" Amy said.

The monks weren't moving quickly, but their gait wasn't the slow shambling of the zombies. Just a steady shuffle. Paul gathered the packs and set them to the side of the road.

"Joe, you and I go for the six up there. Amy, can you take those three?"

"You bet," she said. She spun her bō like a propeller in front of her and advanced on the three hapless monks.

Paul watched her a moment and wished he knew how to do that. He just held his staff as she'd told him, and he and Joe moved against the six. Paul found that the staffs were ideal tools to deal with the monks. They didn't reach out or try to parry the strikes, just kept moving in those three-person formations, trying to separate and surround them.

Paul hit one in the center of the chest, and it went down. As it fell, the hood pulled back and he saw the face--slack-jawed, with sallow skin and black eyes. Paul's skin crawled. Then, with renewed effort, he swung the staff and clubbed another in the head. He swung back and hit the third in the head. All three were down. Then there was a puff of acrid smoke and they were gone--all but the cloaks.

Joe had a little more trouble with his third one, but finally he knocked it down. Nothing was left of the monks now but smoke and crumpled cloaks.

They turned and saw Amy leaving a pile of cloaks and attacking six more monks.

"More!" Paul said. He and Joe ran to Amy's side and the three fought together, making short work of the new arrivals.

Three more stood under the light down the ramp and didn't move.

"That would have been fifteen," Amy said. "If those ladies hadn't warned us, and if we hadn't had a way to fight them, one or more of us might have been turned."

"Should we go take those three out?" Joe asked, pointing to the group at the bottom of the ramp.

"Nah," Paul said. "Leave 'em. If they start moving our way, we can deal with them. Now we know."

Paul used one end of his staff to shift the empty cloaks around. Something glinted. He knelt to get a closer look. There was a pendant nestled in one cloak. He fished it out with the staff.

"Hey, look what I found," he said, the pendant dangling from one end of the staff. "See if there are any more. Just don't touch them!"

They used their staffs and dug through the cloaks. They accounted for one pendant per three cloaks. They laid the pendants on the side of the road under the light.

"Well, I bet the wearer of the pendant is the controller or leader of the threesome," Joe said.

Amy was looking closely at the pendants. "That's an old Celtic knot design, with a three-pronged pitchfork in the middle." She shuddered. "Don't touch them. These belong to the Adversary."

Paul looked at the three monks down the ramp, then glanced up the ramp toward the freeway. No others had arrived.

"Let's kick this stuff into the ditch," he said. "See if we can get a ride."

Joe stood with the sign. A few cars went by. Then nothing. About twenty minutes later, a truck turned up the ramp. It rolled slowly up and pulled over. It was another stake-side flatbed truck. A man with flowing, long black hair jumped out of the driver's side smiling.

"Looks like you met some of the monks," he said laughing. "Nasty, aren't they? Where you heading?"

"Anywhere west," Joe said.

"You're in luck. We're heading to Pine Ridge. I'm Ricky White Feather."

"Where's Pine Ridge?" Paul asked.

"South Dakota," Ricky said. "Indian country. It's a long drive. There's some hay in the back, jump in!"

They climbed in. There were two other people nestled in the hay.

"These are my cousins, Cory and Cody. We don't go too fast, but we'll get there. The Lord God provides," Ricky said.

"The Lord God certainly does," Paul said. He introduced himself and the other two.

Ricky climbed back in the driver's seat and slowly, noisily drove off. The truck was a bit bouncy, but the hay made for a soft place to rest. Cory and Cody nodded off almost immediately.

Joe and Amy followed their example a few minutes later. Paul struggled, though. He wanted to sleep but kept jerking awake thinking more monks were coming at them. The slack, sallow face and black eyes floated in his vision. He jerked awake one more time and looked out the back of the truck. Nothing there but the dark freeway receding behind them.

He bowed his head and prayed, asking for strength for whatever might lie ahead. Finally, sleep came.

CHAPTER ELEVEN
Samurai

THE RISING sun peeked through the slats of the sides of the stake-bed. Paul and the others were warm and comfortable nestled in the hay, but the cool morning air brushed across their faces, leaving a hint of moisture. The truck was bucking around a little more since they'd left the freeway a couple of hours earlier.

Paul stayed where he was, not wanting to move or get up. He felt safe, secure, and warm. He figured they were somewhere in Nebraska by now. Cody and Cory were still asleep, so he didn't have much chance to talk to them. Ricky, for what little Paul had seen of him so far, was very different in manner and looks from the Indians he knew back home. Some of Paul's heritage was Native American and a few of his relatives lived in the old Cherokee villages in the North Carolina mountains.

Then the truck bounced several times and came to a stop.

He heard the driver door slam, and Ricky banged on the side of the bed.

"Wake up, my beauties! Gonna get gas, coffee and breakfast." Ricky came around the back, his big smile on his face. "What a beautiful morning the Lord has made! Let's not waste it, c'mon!"

Paul emerged from the hay, rumpled and with bits of hay stuck to his clothes. Joe and Amy fussed a bit more with shaking out the hay, and then they all picked hay out of each other's hair. Cory, who wore his black hair short, just ran his hands quickly over his head, knocking out most of the hay bits. Cody, whose hair was long like Ricky's, had a bit more work to do.

Paul jumped down from the truck bed, then helped Amy and Joe. They found themselves at a gas station with a McDonald's.

"Another McDonald's," Joe said.

"They're everywhere," Amy said. "Just once, I'd like to see a Wendy's."

"Welcome to Valentine, Nebraska," Ricky said. "Go inside, get something to eat, use the restrooms. I'll be in after I gas up."

"Ricky is almost too upbeat," Joe said, rubbing sleep from his eyes and yawning. "It is too early in the morning for that kind of joyfulness."

Joe, Amy, and Paul held onto their packs and staffs and kept close to each other.

"Boy, you guys are tight," Cory said as they walked across the lot. "Where you from?"

"North Carolina," Paul said.

"That is some trek," Cody said, stripping more hay bits from his hair.

"It's been interesting," Joe said.

Everyone headed to the restrooms first, then they got food and found a table near power.

"Free Wi-Fi!" Amy said.

Cody grinned at her. "Amazing, isn't it? We even have mobile phones."

Amy blushed. "I didn't mean . . . "

"S'okay," Cody said smiling. "Just kidding. We're not on the res, yet. That'll be an education."

They fired up their tablets and connected. Most of the information was the same kind of thing they'd seen before, including the strange events happening at major cities. Newer reports told of roving gangs taking advantage of the chaos and lack of law enforcement and government in metropolitan areas. There were also stories about new odd occurrences, like the plague of frogs. After their experiences so far, Paul thought he could see the Adversary's handiwork across the board. Now, though, the flow of news and information they found online slowed and much of the information was a couple of days old. What they did find that was new centered on the violence and chaos and usually reported on blogs and alternative news sources instead of the standard sources.

"It's just getting worse," Paul said. "People are dying. The government is just gone. Gangs are taking over in the big cities. This is really horrible."

"Yeah," Joe said.

"The Devil is having a heyday," Ricky said, bringing his breakfast to the table. "Somehow, I get the feeling you guys are all tied up in it."

"We're in it, that's correct," Paul said.

"So, you gonna share your story?" Ricky asked.

Paul sat back and looked at the other two. Joe and Amy nodded. So, he told the tale while they ate, with help from Joe and Amy. He left nothing out. There didn't seem to be any point in holding back at this stage.

Cory and Cody listened with eyes wide.

"Zombies?" Cory said. "Really?"

"Yeah," Joe said. "They really slimed up our friend's car."

"It's been a long, strange trip, for sure," Paul said.

"Well, we're Indians," Ricky said, his pronunciation sounding like "in-dins." "We live outside the mainstream, for the most part, so we watched this from the outside looking in."

"You're what? I thought you looked Native American," Joe said.

"Indian, yeah," Ricky said, grinning at Joe. "But I notice that cities are being attacked. The little places are pretty much left alone."

"Well, except the plague of frogs," Paul said. "That was a small town."

"And you're seeing a coyote with glowing eyes," Ricky said. "You know, in our culture, the coyote is a significant figure. Depending on the story, he's either the trickster, or he's a messenger from the Great Spirit. This, where the coyote is the embodiment of the Adversary, is significant. I'm not sure how, though."

"I don't think he's just a trickster," Paul said. "He's the Adversary, and he's made all this happen. I don't mean any disrespect."

"None taken," Ricky said, waving off the comment. "This just twists our world view a little. I'm a Christian, but I do embrace my cultural heritage too. And I'm fascinated that an angel came to you."

"Gabriel is just a messenger," Paul smiled. "At least, that's what he keeps telling us."

"I wish Gabriel would show up again," Amy said. "Things seem safer when he's around."

"Well, at least you're far enough away from Des Moines not to have to worry about monks anymore," Ricky said. "I heard in the last couple of days, the monks had turned about half of the population there, and they weren't slowing down. That's bad."

"Yeah," Amy said. She reached in her pack and pulled out a notepad. She sketched what she remembered of the pendant design on a page and showed it to the others. "Have you seen this before, or do you know what it means?"

"We're thinking the pendants with this design were worn by the leader or controller of each group of three," Paul said. "Only one was found with every three cloaks. At least, with the ones we fought, anyway."

"Hmm," Ricky said, "that's new." He looked at the drawing a moment. "It looks kind of Celtic, but with a devil's fork. You didn't touch any of these, did you?"

"No," Joe said. "We fished them out with our sticks. No one wanted to touch any of that."

"Good." Ricky sat back and thought for a moment. "I'm going to call a friend near Des Moines and share some of this with him. It might help them better fight this monk thing."

He got up and went outside.

"How long to Pine Ridge?" Paul asked Cory and Cody.

"Couple of hours, I think," Cory said.

"And then Rapid City is another couple of hours past that," Paul said. "That's where we can get on I-90. What do you think our chances are of hitchhiking out of Pine Ridge?"

"Probably not great," Cody said. "Should talk to Ricky about it. He might know someone heading west from there."

"Let's get out to the truck," Paul said, cleaning up the trash from his meal. "We'll see if Ricky has an idea."

Paul was helping Amy get herself and their packs into the back of the truck when he heard something behind him. He turned. Three figures approached from the other side of the gas station. They wore colorful, enameled leather armor and huge, ornate mask helmets, and had curved swords and knives tucked into their belts.

"Um, Amy," he said, pointing.

Amy looked. "Samurai!" she said in an incredulous tone.

The three were in no hurry, just marching toward them. They seemed to be focused on Paul. He shifted to the other side of the truck, and the samurai changed direction slightly, tracking him. He ran quickly back to the other side of the truck, and the samurai changed direction again, straight for him.

"I'm going to draw them off you guys," he said tossing his pack and staff into the truck. He turned and jogged away toward the road. When he looked back, the samurai were jogging after him. Their armor clattered and made running clumsy and difficult for them.

I wonder how good their cardio training is, Paul thought. He kicked it up to his mile pace. After a while, he looked back. The samurai were still following, but flagging and flailing about and losing ground. Paul slowed so they wouldn't give up completely.

When he next looked back, the truck was closing in behind the samurai. Joe and Amy stood in the back, armed with their staffs. As the truck rolled up, they whacked two of the samurai in the back of the helmets and knocked them down. The third samurai drew his katana and tried to charge Paul, but he was winded and shaky and stumbled a lot. Paul circled around at an easy pace, leading the samurai, while Joe and Amy prepared an ambush. As he led the samurai by the truck, both Joe and Amy attacked from behind and hammered against his helmet with staffs, sending the helmet rolling into the ditch. One more swipe with Joe's staff connected solidly against the side of the samurai's head. He went down in a clattering heap. Paul didn't get a good look at the samurai without his helmet, but he noticed it was bald, with the same sallow skin he'd seen on the monks.

Ricky came running around the truck, just as the three samurai evaporated into a caustic cloud of smoke that blew away in the morning breeze.

"That was too much like the monks," Paul said, breathing heavily. "Don't touch any of their stuff. Joe, use your staff and see if there's anything similar to the monk pendants inside these piles."

Amy and Joe used their staffs to flip and sort through the armor and weapons. The only thing they found was a design etched into the base of the blades of the katanas, wakizashis, and tantos. It was the three-pronged fork.

"Later period infantry-style samurai," Amy said. "They only had swords."

"At least the town wasn't full of these," Paul said, kicking the armor and weapons into the ditch. "The Adversary seems to know where we are. And these guys were coming for me specifically."

"Well, you are chosen," Ricky said. "If you fail, it all fails. Of course the Adversary will target you. If you die, he wins."

"I don't want to die, not yet."

"We don't want you to, either." Amy's face was set.

Ricky headed to the truck. "Let's get going before any more appear."

CHAPTER TWELVE
Black Fog

"SO THE monks and the samurai all had something with the three-prong fork symbol," Paul said as they bounced in the back of Ricky's truck. "And they all move and work in threes. So how is the Adversary tracking us?"

"You mean tracking you," Cody said, laughing. "We Indians just blend into the background, en'it?"

"Yeah, cousin!" Cory said. Then he looked curiously at Paul. "You look a bit Indian yourself, but you're all mixed up--buffalo hair, dark eyes and tan."

Paul smiled. "Mom is black and Carolina Cherokee. Dad's family is Irish."

"I've been thinking," Amy said suddenly, shifting in the hay to get comfortable. "Every time we get online at McD's or someplace, we get something like frogs, monks, or samurai. The zombies in Asheville weren't like that; they seemed more like the other events hitting St. Louis, Charlotte and Washington, D.C. The truck stop in Knoxville, we didn't get online. I don't even remember if they had wireless."

"I was starting to think that the appearance of the coyote would predict weird stuff," Paul said. "But I haven't seen him in a while. I think your theory makes more sense."

"Yeah," Joe said. "Let's be more careful with the tablets from now on."

"That may make the coyote show up again," Paul said.

"If he does, we may at least learn something new about the

Adversary's plan or what's going on," Amy said.

Paul thought for a moment. "We may not want to go by way of Rapid City. I looked up the route from Pine Ridge to there just before we shut down and left Micky-D's. If the Adversary's been tracking our movements online, he may have some nasty plan in place somewhere along there. Especially now that we eliminated his samurai."

"What way should we go, then?" Amy asked.

"I don't know," Paul said. "We need another map. The one I got in North Carolina only covered up to the Mississippi. We've been running on good guesses and God's grace since."

"New map, watch for three-pronged forks, don't go online," Amy summed up. "Anything else we need to do when we get to Pine Ridge?"

"Find a ride," Joe said.

#

Paul watched the landscape roll by between the slats of the truck bed's wooden sides. He had never been this far from home before, and without his parents. He felt lost and vulnerable. Even with Joe and Amy to help, he didn't know how he would complete the mission. He pressed his face against the slats and gripped one of the boards.

The country was strange to him, and so were the people. Still, they seemed to be what God had provided to help them on their way. He just wished he knew better what he was doing and where he was going. Tears threatened to spill from his eyes and his throat constricted. He closed his eyes and pulled in a slow, deep breath.

Father, he prayed silently, I depend on Your grace and love to get me through. I thank You for Joe and Amy, too. Please look after my family and keep them safe until the mission is completed. I look to You for the strength, wisdom, and understanding to do as You require. I only want to serve You. Help us keep to the right path. I ask this in Your Son's name, Jesus Christ. Amen.

Paul had a better handle on his emotions after the prayer and felt some relief. He stole a quick glance at Joe and Amy. They were talking quietly and looking out the other side of the truck. The last thing he needed was to have them witness his near breakdown.

#

The main intersection in Pine Ridge had a gas station/convenience store/café and a welcome center. Ricky parked the truck in front of the cafe and went inside while Paul, Joe, and Amy waited outside with Cory and Cody.

As soon as they arrived, they heard disturbing news about a black fog over Rapid City. It sounded like the same black fog that had settled over Washington, D.C. People gathered in front of the store talking and listening to a radio report. Paul moved closer to better hear, with Joe and Amy close behind. According to the newscast on the radio, witnesses reported that no one had come out of the city since the fog descended, and the fog was creeping south toward Pine Ridge.

"Pine Ridge needs to be evacuated," Paul said, trying to get the attention of the adults listening to the report. "That fog is the same that came down on the capital."

A couple of the adults looked at Paul, but then they turned away and went back to talking among themselves.

Paul looked at Joe and Amy. "The Adversary is sending the black fog! These people need to get out while they can."

"It's okay, Paul," Cody said, putting a hand on his shoulder and gently pulling him away. "They don't know you. They do know Ricky, and they'll listen to him."

Frustrated, Paul went to the convenience store and bought a map that covered the western half of the U.S. Outside, he gathered Joe and Amy to study it. They determined their best shot would be to head west to Wyoming and catch I-90 around Sundance.

"We'll need to go soon," Paul said. "The fog coming south could cut off the route before we get to Hot Springs. We don't know what this fog does, but I bet we can't fight it with our staffs."

"Wish Ricky would come out and let us know what's going on," Joe said.

Amy kept looking at the map. "I wish we weren't in this crisis," she said. "I'd like to see Mt. Rushmore, Crazy Horse, and some of the other sites around the Black Hills."

"Lessee, we're running for our lives, the Adversary is out to get us. And our dear Amy here, she wants to go sightseeing." Joe grinned, then ducked away as Amy took a swipe at him. He looked at his staff. It was scraped and scarred, and the ends were rounded from use. "Think we should leave these?"

"Absolutely not," Paul said. "I'm betting we'll need them again."

"Oh, yes," Amy said. "They're wood and provide a kind of insulation between us and others, like the monks. Never know when they'll be useful."

The crowd of adults were still talking. Ricky hadn't come out yet. Paul grew nervous.

"We need to move," he said. "Let's pray, then see what leads us."

The three prayed in a huddle. Paul begged for safe travels and God's blessing on them. Amy asked that their location and direction be hidden from the Adversary. Joe prayed for strength and the ability to overcome any opponents the Adversary sent against them.

As they wrapped up, Ricky came out of the café. For once, he wasn't smiling.

"Okay," he said, "I have a cousin heading to Sundance, over in Wyoming, and he'll take you there. He's going to take the south route, rather than go by Rapid City and the freeway. He's a little upset about that. He has a lady friend in Rapid City. But he'll leave in a few minutes."

"Thanks, Ricky," Paul said. "I think you should try to evacuate Pine Ridge. We don't know what this fog does. It seems like the same fog that covered Washington, D.C. If no one is here when it arrives, no one dies. And the Adversary gets no information from anyone here."

"That's what we're going to do. I have enough pull around here that we can make this happen." Ricky pointed to an older sedan across the parking lot. "That's my cousin Mark's car. You guys can load up now. I know it doesn't look like much, but Mark takes good care of it and it runs great. I hope you guys make it. I'll be praying for you. A lot of people will be praying for you."

"Again, thanks, Ricky," Paul said. "You've been a great help."

After hugs and handshakes, the three got their stuff into Mark's car. Mark, an older, larger, stockier man, with his long hair braided, came out and introduced himself.

"If what I'm hearing is true," he said, "we shouldn't waste any more time. Let's go."

#

They passed the turnoff to BIA Highway 41, also called Little Man Road. That would have taken them north toward Rapid City. Paul scanned the horizon to the north and saw a faint black shadow in the distance.

"I think I see it," he said, and nodded to the others. "It's a good thing we left when we did."

"Wish we could get my Rosa," Mark said. "I'm afraid for her."

"Mark," Paul said, "Gabriel told me that my mission will restore the world. I can only hope he meant that we will have all our families back."

"Me, too," Mark said.

"All I can do is keep trying," Paul said, "and praying."

Mark asked questions of the three periodically as they drove. When he got an answer, he would go silent for a while. Then, after a bit, he'd ask another question and go through the same process.

After driving across the broad farmlands of western South Dakota, they turned northwest on US 385.

"This is bringing us closer to Rapid City," Amy said.

"No worries," Mark said. "We swing west to the other side of the Black Hills soon."

Mark wasn't poking along, though. Hot Springs wasn't far. Paul kept a lookout on the horizon to the north. As they approached Hot Springs, the black shadow made the horizon fuzzy again. At Hot Springs, Mark took the US 18 bypass.

The black fog crept over the hills north of Hot Springs as they rolled along the bypass.

"That's getting pretty close," he said, pointing. Mark merged onto US 18 proper just as black fog started flowing over a nearby hill.

Joe was asleep, with the rear window rolled down and his arm resting in it. Paul looked back and saw wisps of the black fog trailing after the car, some even touching it.

"Amy, get Joe inside and get his window rolled up!"

Amy grabbed Joe just as a wisp reached through and touched his arm. Joe jerked awake, eyes wide and mouth open in a soundless scream. His body spasmed and shook. Amy pulled him over and quickly rolled up his window. Mark sped up and they drove into the rolling country of the Black Hills, leaving the black fog behind.

Joe lay across the back seat, his head on Amy's lap, writhing in silent agony.

CHAPTER THIRTEEN
Aliens

THEY OUTRAN the black fog and made it to US 85. Heading north, they hoped to make I-90 before more obstacles and dangers were placed in their way.

Joe was breathing easy now, no longer writhing and jerking. Amy examined his right arm where the wisp of fog had touched it. "There's a red welt about three inches long near his elbow," she reported.

Mark was extremely upset, seeing what a faint touch of a wisp of the fog could do.

"Oh, those poor people in Rapid City," he said. "My poor Rosa. They all must either be dead or in incredible agony."

They were passing the small town of Newcastle when Joe started to rouse. He moaned a little, then tried to sit up. Amy helped get him in a sitting position. Joe automatically cradled his right arm.

"Man, what happened?" he asked. "My arm feels like it's been on fire."

"A wisp of that black fog touched you," Amy said.

"Just a wisp? Wow, that stuff packs a punch." He took a couple of deep breaths and looked down at his arm. "I think I know what Hell would be like now."

Paul turned back into his seat, relieved that Joe was recovering. A tension left him. What would he do without Joe watching his back?

#

At Sundance, Mark dropped them off on the ramp for west I-90.

"Devil's Tower is just north of here," Joe said as they walked up the ramp. "That's where they had the alien contact in that old movie, something-something-third-kind."

"Well, we don't need any close encounters. We had too many of those already," Amy said, then stopped. "What is this?"

A grate of wide-spaced metal bars crossed the road.

"I think this is called a cow guard or something like that," Paul said. "It's supposed to keep animals from getting on the freeway. They see it and don't want to step on it."

Joe eyed it suspiciously. "I don't want to step on it, either."

"I think it's all right," Paul said. He made his way across. "See? Just put your heel on one bar and your toe on the next one."

They all crossed the cattle guard without incident and walked up the ramp a way. There wasn't much shoulder and they had to drop their packs in the gravel.

The afternoon wore on and only a handful of cars had come up the ramp.

"Hey, Amy," Joe said, "how about if you show me some of your bō fighting techniques?"

"How do you think your arm will hold up?" Amy asked.

He waved it in front of her. "Feeling loose and already better."

She showed him some basic techniques and drilled him on them until he knew them well. Then they sparred. Paul enjoyed the show until Amy accidentally bounced her staff off Joe's elbow.

Joe collapsed on the road, gasping in pain.

"Okay," he managed to say. "Time out."

"I'm sorry, Joe," Amy said, kneeling next to him. "I didn't mean to hit there."

He sat up, then after a while stood and shook out his arm.

"It's okay, Amy," he said. "I'll heal."

"We should move further up," Paul said, shaking his head at the other two. "We need to get up on the main part of the freeway before dark. There's traffic up there. After dark, they won't be able to see us."

"Then after dark, we move back down here near the light?" Amy asked.

"Well, theoretically, yes. But I hope we'll have a ride by then."

"We aren't getting any business down here," Joe said. "Let's go."

They picked up their gear, hiked up to the interstate, and set up on the shoulder in a visible location. Joe took a turn with his thumb out. After about fifteen minutes, an older sedan pulled over.

"Hop in," the driver of the sedan said. "Got lots of room."

"We're heading into northwestern Montana," Paul said.

"Well, I can take you as far as Hardin. That should help," the driver said. "I'm Richard."

Paul remembered seeing Hardin on the map, not far from the southern border of Montana. Why did their progress have to be so agonizingly slow? Then he felt guilty for not being grateful they made any progress at all.

#

The dark was complete and Richard, the driver, wasn't much of a talker. Paul watched the occasional vehicle lights pass on the eastbound lanes. Once in a while, a lone yard light would glow softly off in the distance, providing the only evidence of human habitation in the rugged Wyoming countryside. The city of Gillette had been a brief cluster of sparkling lights along the freeway.

Their approach to another Wyoming town, Buffalo, was announced by a sign.

"I'm going to stop there for gas," Richard said. "I could probably make it to Sheridan, but let's not chance it."

"Sounds good," Paul said.

Amy poked Joe to wake him up. "We're going to stop soon."

Richard pulled into a gas station across from a Holiday Inn Express and started to fill up the car. Paul, Joe, and Amy went inside to use the facilities and get some drinks. They had their packs and staffs, so things were a little clumsy, but they managed. They stood outside waiting for Richard. He finished with the car and went inside to pay for gas.

"I'm going to make a pit stop, too. I'll be out in a few minutes," he said as he went through the door.

The three walked out to the car. Paul looked up and down the road and around the area.

"The samurai have you spooked, eh?" Joe asked.

"Yeah, and the black fog. That stuff was terrifying, but you know that."

Joe nodded agreement. Amy looked wistfully at the Holiday Inn across the road.

"I wish we could get rooms and stay a night or two there. A warm bed, hot shower, and breakfast in the morning."

"Well," Paul pointed down the road, "there's a Motel 6 just up there. We could get one room, take shifts on the bed and shower, and get no breakfast."

"I think the Motel 6 still busts our budget," Joe said.

"You're right," Paul agreed. "I'm hoping we have enough to at least eat once in a while until we get this mission accomplished."

"Will we at least be able to get showers soon?" Amy asked.

"Last time we were online, I did see that Billings had one of those Pilot truck stops, so I think we can get showers there."

"We just have to get there," Joe said.

Yes, Paul thought, *we just have to get there.*

A light caught his eye just above the town of Buffalo. It was changing color and blinking, like an aircraft light, but it seemed too low to be an aircraft. It was moving their direction.

"Hey, guys, look at . . . " Paul said.

Just as he spoke, the light grew to a large, disk-shaped object and beams shot out of the sides of it. The beams hit buildings, cars and trucks, causing explosions and turning them into flame and slag.

"A flying saucer!" Joe yelled.

The saucer blasted away a building and some cars next to the Holiday Inn. Legs appeared out of the base of the object and it landed amid the rubble it had just created. A ramp dropped down and light flooded out from the inside of the craft. Figures carrying short sticks trotted down the ramp directly toward the gas station. They were only about four feet tall. As they approached, Paul could see they looked like the classic "little green men" of comic book science fiction. Big eyes, oval head, funny hands. The lead aliens pointed their sticks and blasted away a couple cars.

"Run!" Paul yelled. He led the way to a building on the other side of the gas station. *Oh, God, help us,* he prayed as they ran. *How will we fight these guys?*

From the cover of the building, Paul looked around the corner to get a look at what was going on. Richard's car exploded into a ball of fire, as did three other vehicles at the pumps. Then the aliens trained their sticks on the building and the windows blew out as the store exploded in a huge fireball.

"Richard's gone," Paul said. "So is everyone else there. We have to get on the flank or behind these guys. We need one of their sticks."

Joe nodded. "They don't seem to be working in threes like the others. I count eight." He pointed at a huge propane tank at the other end of the building. "And we don't want to go that way."

Paul looked around. "Let's get to the other side of that steak house," he said, nodding toward the small restaurant behind them. "We can do that without being seen."

They raced across the lot and behind the steak house. There they found a place to take cover and see what was happening. The aliens now closed on the building they had first stopped behind.

"While they're focused there, I'm going to get in that ditch by the road. Give me your packs, I'll stow them there. You two get over behind those vehicles and concrete barriers. As soon as we can get behind or on a flank and can take one out, we'll go for it."

Paul grabbed the packs and sprinted to the ditch as Joe and Amy melted into a cluster of vehicles and Jersey barriers.

From the ditch, Paul could see the aliens moving slowly. He crept along, staff in hand, his movement concealed from the aliens. One of the aliens came close, but was focused on the steak house, as were the others. He was close enough, Paul could take him without the others seeing, he thought.

Gripping his staff, Paul leaped silently from the ditch, whacked the alien on the back of the head, and grabbed its stick as the alien crumpled to the ground.

Paul jumped back into the ditch and examined the stick. It was just two feet long, felt like plastic, and hummed and vibrated in his hands. He glanced at the remaining aliens to figure out how to hold it, then looked back at his own stick. There was a button on the side near one end that must fire it.

Paul stood, pointed the stick at one of the aliens and pushed the button, praying that he was pointing the stick in the right direction. The stick tried to jump out of his hands, but a beam shot out and vaporized the alien.

Two down, six to go. He ducked down into the ditch and moved back to where he had stashed the packs. He popped up and fired again, vaporizing another alien. As he did so, Amy and Joe moved against two others who were now focused on Paul. Paul ducked back into the ditch just as two beams shot over his head. He could feel the heat of the beams from a couple of yards away.

Amy and Joe should have downed their two aliens, Paul thought. He peeked up to see what was going on and saw Amy burn down an alien. Joe was having trouble sorting out the stick.

Get down, Joe, Paul thought. *Get behind the barrier.*

Joe leaped for the Jersey barrier and Amy turned to take aim at another alien. Paul jumped out of the ditch to fire.

Both remaining aliens went down, but not before firing at Joe.

CHAPTER FOURTEEN

Loss

PAUL RAN across the parking lot. Fear made him shaky. Had the aliens made a direct hit? He'd seen the sticks vaporize the aliens, and he'd felt the heat from the beams. What would the beams do to humans?

He could see Joe's feet sticking out from behind the barrier. Amy was bent over Joe when Paul got there. Paul couldn't see past her.

"Is he okay?" Paul asked.

Amy turned and shook her head. There were tears in her eyes.

Paul stepped closer. Joe lay there with most of his left side burned off from above his waist to his neck. There wasn't much blood. Joe's face was frozen in a pained expression.

Paul's legs turned to rubber and he fell on his knees next to Joe. Then the smell of burnt flesh hit him and he had to turn and vomit. Amy lurched over the barrier and vomited too.

Behind him, Paul could hear the sounds of the saucer blasting things across the street. He wiped his mouth. He could feel tears streamed down his cheeks, but he didn't have time to cry now. He stood and picked up one of the sticks.

Amy did too. Tears had left tracks down her dirty cheeks, but her face was set in a look Paul had seen before, when she was fighting monks.

They jogged toward the saucer, skirting the gas station inferno. Paul didn't know what the sticks' range was, but based on how the aliens used them, he guessed they should be effective by the time they were adjacent to the far end of the Holiday Inn. He took a few more steps for good measure, then aimed the stick at the saucer and pushed the button. Amy did the same.

The sides of the saucer glowed, lights flickered, and suddenly the saucer disappeared. Air in the vicinity rushed into the empty space the saucer had once occupied. The sticks in their hands ceased to hum and vibrate. Paul pointed his at the ground and pushed the button. Nothing happened.

Holding onto the stick, he walked back to where they'd left Joe. Amy followed. On the way, he kicked at a couple of the piles of alien ashes. There were no amulets among the debris other than the remains of the weapon sticks.

Paul knelt beside the body of his best friend. Ignoring the smell of burnt flesh, he reached out and touched Joe's face. Gently, as he'd seen in countless movies and TV shows, he closed his friend's eyes.

"We're done, aren't we?" Paul asked no one in particular, tears tracking down his cheeks. "It's all finished. We can't complete this mission. The Adversary beat us."

"No, Paul!" Amy said behind him.

"He was my best friend, Amy! I can't go on without him."

"You have me," she said quietly and put her hand on his shoulder.

He sat back on his heels and looked at her. "Sorry. I didn't mean it like that."

"I know."

"What are we going to do?"

"You must complete the mission," a voice said.

Paul got to his feet, turned, and saw Gabriel.

"But we lost Joe," Paul said. "How can we keep going? He's my best friend and he had my back. I can't go on without him. He's only fourteen years old and they killed him! They killed him!" Paul wiped his face with his hands and felt the tears smearing the grime on his skin. "Oh, man, what are we going to tell his parents? This is too big for us."

"How can you not go on?" Gabriel gently picked up Joe's body. "So much depends on you and Joe gave his life for this mission. You can't let his sacrifice go for nothing. He saved your life. He saved it more than once and in many ways. Yes, that is what a loving and devoted friend does. He did not make this sacrifice to have you give up. He would expect you to complete the mission."

Paul stared at Gabriel. He knew in his heart that the angel was right. He couldn't let Joe's death be the end of it. His parents, and Amy's and Joe's, were trapped in Charlotte, at the mercy of the Adversary, and the rest of the world was in turmoil. He couldn't quit, he knew.

"You always have a tough message for me, don't you, Gabriel?" Paul said. He looked down at Joe, ashamed of the anger now.

"Yes, Paul," Gabriel said. "I am the Lord God's messenger. That is what I do."

"And I must complete my mission," Paul said. He closed his eyes and offered up a prayer. Then he opened his eyes, looked at Joe, and said a silent goodbye to him.

"I'll take care of Joe," the angel said. "He is one of the Lord God's beloved children."

Then Gabriel disappeared along with Joe's body.

Amy looked at Paul in silence a moment, then stooped to pick up the alien stick she'd dropped.

"The aliens better not come back," she said, her gray eyes burning in the starlit night.

Paul turned and walked to the ditch where he'd stashed the packs. Joe's pack was gone. He'd half expected that. He picked up his pack and put the alien stick in it, then located his staff. Amy woodenly followed Paul's lead.

"Let's get back to the freeway, Amy," Paul said, reaching for her hand, then led the way back to the freeway. He felt like he was walking through a surreal landscape by that one painter, he didn't remember his name. Just ten minutes ago, they were all waiting at the gas station to get back into the car, and now Joe was gone, and the gas station was burning. The steakhouse was still standing, though.

He looked back as he walked slowly to see Amy trailed along behind. She's still here, too, he thought.

The interchange was dark. There were a few lights, but they didn't shine on the ramp. Paul and Amy set up as close to the light as they could.

Paul could see police and emergency vehicle lights around the gas station blaze.

"I wonder what they're going to make of all that," Amy said, looking back to the town.

"Don't know," Paul said. "Unless there were other witnesses from the hotel or steakhouse, there isn't much to work with."

"If there are other witnesses, we better hope to be gone before someone mentions us walking away."

Paul stuck out his thumb as a car came up from the other direction and turned up the ramp. It pulled over and he trotted up to the passenger window.

"We're heading to Billings," Paul said.

"Hop in," said the woman driver. Paul couldn't see much in the dark, but she wore her hair short and her voice was soft and gentle. "So am I."

Paul followed Amy into the back seat and they settled in as the woman accelerated up the ramp.

"I'm Jennifer," the woman said. "I'm a minister at a church in Billings. I've been visiting my parents on their farm just east of here. Where are you two from?"

Paul introduced himself and Amy and explained where they were from.

"You're a minister, eh?" Paul asked. "Think you're up for a very strange story?"

Jennifer laughed. Paul could see part of her face through the rear view mirror and thought she had a nice smile.

"Does it have something to do with all the strange stuff going on?" she said. "Sure."

Paul started off explaining why they were on the road and what had happened so far. Amy filled in some, adding her own particular feelings and experiences. They told everything, but struggled and stumbled over what happened in Buffalo and the loss of Joe. Joe wasn't there to add his part. Paul and Amy felt the reality of the situation hitting hard.

Paul swallowed hard. "He was my best friend."

"Yeah," Amy agreed. "I miss him."

Jennifer slowed and pulled the car onto the shoulder. She turned on the emergency flashers.

"You're not going to kick us out, are you?" Amy asked.

"Oh, no, dear," Jennifer said, turning in her seat after untangling from the seatbelt. "I'm going to pray with you."

She reached her arms over the seat, took their hands, then began praying. Through his closed eyelids Paul could see the emergency flashers blinking.

"Father," Jennifer said, her voice thick with tears, "please help us understand it is not about Amy. It is not about Paul. It is not about poor Joe. It is about Jesus Christ and our salvation. Keep these young people strong."

Paul and Amy sobbed and cried into each other's shoulders then, and Jennifer put her hands on their heads.

As Paul and Amy recovered, Jennifer held their hands quietly, and they could feel the love and care she tried to share.

"Thank you so much," Amy said.

"Yes, thank you," Paul added. "We needed that."

Jennifer turned around, buckled in, and got the car back on the freeway. She didn't make them talk, and Paul was grateful.

A little over two hours later, she left the freeway.

"I'm taking you guys to my house," she said. "I have a couple of extra rooms and you can rest there. You both look like you could use a little break."

"Are you sure?" Paul asked. "We tend to attract bad things."

"I wouldn't worry about that," Jennifer said. "We are well in the arms of Jesus, and the Adversary has no allies in my home."

Jennifer's house was modest and she herded Paul and Amy to small rooms with comfy beds and showed them the facilities.

"I have work to do at the church this morning," she said. "I'll be out for a couple of hours. You two get some rest."

Paul let Amy shower first. When she left the bathroom, she went straight to her bed without bothering to shut the door. By the time Paul finished showering, Amy was sleeping.

Paul quietly shut her door, then went to his own room. He was asleep as soon as his head hit the pillow.

#

Paul woke to the smell of maple, apples, and cinnamon. Pleasant voices drifted up through the floor. Another scent hit his nose--coffee. Hot, black, rich coffee. He must be dreaming. He took a deep breath and stretched--and heard the voices and laughter again. Then he noticed the pillow under his head, and the warm, soft bed beneath him.

He opened his eyes. The first thing he saw was the alien stick poking out from one side of his backpack. The aliens . . . the explosions . . . Joe.

His backpack was in rough shape--stained and dirty, especially around the bottom, from sitting on the ground and being dragged through gravel and dirt. The zippers were open and clothes hung from the pouches. His staff leaned against the wall next to the pack, dirty and scarred from being used as a weapon.

It all came back. They were in Jennifer's house--Jennifer, the fortyish woman they had just met, a minister at a Billings, Montana church, who'd who picked them up in the middle of the night on a dark country freeway, and who'd just let them stay at her home.

Paul got up, dressed, and visited the bathroom. When he found his way into the kitchen, Amy and Jennifer were there, with Jennifer cooking, talking, and laughing softly. The warm kitchen, the food and coffee smells, the women's pleasant voices, all combined to bring a smile to Paul's face.

"There he is!" Jennifer said. "Sit down. I have a nice meal ready for you." She brought a large, heavy plate with sausage links, eggs, and apple pancakes.

Paul buttered the pancakes, poured maple syrup over them, and dug in. He listened to Amy and Jennifer talking and telling stories. Sometimes he laughed in spite of himself. Then he'd look to his side where Joe should be and remember.

Jennifer noticed.

"Paul, Joe is with Jesus now. From what Amy's told me, you can be sure of that." She came around the table, kissed his cheek, and hugged him. "He'll be waiting for you someday, safe in blessed peace with our Savior, and you'll have lots to tell each other."

"It's just hard," Paul said, then looked at Amy. "He's always been there, he and Amy. We've always been best friends."

"I can't remember a time in our lives we haven't been together," Amy said. "I just assumed we always would be together. I miss Joe."

"You guys are rare," Jennifer said. "Few people are able to grow up and be as close as you three have been. You are very blessed. Be thankful for the time you've had."

Paul's plate was clean. Jennifer grabbed it and went to the stove.

"What do you want for seconds?" she asked.

"More of those wonderful pancakes?" Paul said. "A couple more sausages?"

"Order up!" she said, and brought back the plate with what he'd requested.

Paul noticed a ring on her left hand.

"You're married?" he asked.

"Was. My husband died several years ago," she said as she started cleaning up, turning away from them. "He was a wonderful husband and father. He and my daughter were killed by a drunk driver."

"That's awful," Amy said as she got up to help clear dishes.

"Yes, it was. My faith, though . . . well, I know that they are with Jesus and I'll be with them again someday. It took some time to come to grips with that." She turned back to the kids. "I know it's hard. But don't let the loss of Joe turn you back. Stay on the mission. More than you know depends on your success."

She took a deep breath. "One of the Bible passages I keep repeating to myself when things get tough is Jeremiah 29:11. *"For I know the plans I have for you,"* declares the LORD, *"plans to prosper you and not to harm you, plans to give you hope and a future.""* Keep your faith in God. Keep on the path. Keep on the mission."

"The Lord God provides," Paul said.

"Yes," Jennifer said. "Yes, He does."

"We could never have come this far without God's provision and support," Amy said. "Paul tries to be so stoic and strong, but I know he is so very dependent on God."

Paul smiled, cheeks full of the last of his pancakes. He got up and brought his plate and silverware to the sink. He glanced at the clock. "We just had breakfast at three in the afternoon. We really should get going."

"Are you sure?" asked Jennifer. "I was going to offer another night's stay."

Paul looked around at Jennifer's comfortable home. It was so good to be around real furniture and eat a home-cooked meal. After all they'd been through, especially with the loss of Joe, he thought, didn't they deserve another night to rest and recoup?

He was already shaking his head, pushing off the temptation. "We need to move on. Like you said, more than we know depends on our success."

CHAPTER FIFTEEN

Caught!

JENNIFER DROVE them to the freeway. They waved as she drove away.

Amy closed her eyes. When she opened them again, she said, "I just prayed for her. She was such a blessing. I feel so much better and some of the dread of the past few days is gone."

Billings spread along the Yellowstone River with farms and ranches close by, and broad, rugged Montana country north and south. Paul breathed deep of the clear late afternoon air, wishing they had more time and less desperate need. This was beautiful country, and Yellowstone National Park was not far. He wished he could go there.

As it was, he only had his thumb out for about fifteen minutes when a car pulled up and offered them a ride.

Sherman was a heavyset man with close-cropped dark hair. He didn't smile much, Paul noticed through the mirror. Paul gave him some details about where they were from and that they needed to get to Choteau. That's when Sherman started asking questions.

"So how do a couple kids your age get all the way out here from North Carolina?"

"It hasn't been easy," Paul said.

"Aren't your parents looking for you?"

"Well, our parents are trapped in Charlotte," Amy said. She proceeded to tell Sherman about how all their parents were duped into going to Charlotte, then trapped when the dome appeared over the city.

"I've been hearing some strange stories about things like that happening," Sherman said. "Washington, D.C. is supposed to be trapped in some black fog."

"So is Rapid City," Paul said. "We saw some of it."

"Well, as far as D.C. is concerned, they can all stay trapped in that fog," he said. "Most of those reports are all nonsense. I bet it is all some kind of liberal plot."

"It is a plot," Paul said, "but maybe not what you are thinking."

"Oh, you never know. Those liberals are pretty creative."

Amy started to reply, but Paul laid his hand on hers and he gave a small shake of his head. This wasn't worth pursuing.

Paul tried to keep conversation on more neutral topics and enjoyed the scenery until late afternoon turned to early evening and twilight. Stars started popping out and Paul got Amy to look out his side window. There were small curtains of Northern Lights dancing in the clear, star-filled northern sky.

As it got full dark, the occasional yard lights blinked on for the scattered farms and ranches. After they passed through some hill country, the land opened up and they could see the lights of Malstrom Air Force Base and then Great Falls.

Sherman cruised down the broad boulevard that was 10th Avenue in Great Falls until he pulled into a restaurant parking lot.

"Well, I turn here," he said pointing to the intersection ahead. He got out of the car, as did Paul and Amy. "You kids keep going down this main drag here, and you'll get to I-15. Head north from there, but not far. You want to get on US 89. That'll take you right up to Choteau."

"Thanks, Sherman, we really appreciated the ride," Paul said.

"So what's so important at Choteau?"

"I have something I'm supposed to do there," Paul said as he got his arms into the straps of his pack.

"Huh," Sherman said. "Well, good luck."

Amy and Paul started walking down the boulevard, they waved at Sherman, who stood watching for a minute. He then turned and went into the restaurant.

After a block or so, Paul looked back at where Sherman had left them. His car was gone.

"I'm a little uneasy about him," he said.

"Me, too."

#

Paul and Amy walked down 10th Avenue, block after block. They passed auto dealers, hardware stores, and restaurants. Finally, there was a Dairy Queen.

"Let's get something," Paul said. "Breakfast at Jennifer's was a long time ago."

They got inside and ordered some burger meals. Amy used the restroom while Paul waited for the food. He noticed police cars went by frequently on the street.

"You get a lot of police patrols here?" he asked the boy behind the counter. He seemed about Paul's age.

"Not usually," the boy said.

"Seems to be a lot of them going up and down the avenue."

The boy just shrugged and pushed a tray toward him. "Your order's ready."

Paul took the food and found a table. He had a funny feeling about those police. Amy came back and sat across from him, setting her pack on a chair nearby.

"I think Sherman called the cops on us," Paul said in a whisper. "Watch the avenue. Seems like a lot of patrols are out there all of a sudden."

When four police cars drove down the avenue in just a few minutes, Amy nodded agreement.

"What do you think we should do?" she asked.

"Let's finish our food--fast, but not too fast. We don't want to attract any attention. Then we'll slip out the side door, get a couple of blocks away from the avenue, and travel parallel to it."

It was hard to chew and swallow through his meal with that pit of dread in his stomach. More than anything, right now Paul wished for a leisurely meal and a chance to rest. When would this mission end?

#

The decision to go in a couple of blocks off the main avenue had seemed like a good one, but Paul felt horribly conspicuous as they moved along 8th Avenue. He and Amy were the only people out moving around at this hour, except for the occasional car. Fortunately, he thought they would be able to identify police vehicles and find cover before they were discovered. He and Amy moved quickly and quietly along the tree-lined street, past houses that were mostly dark.

At one point, the street ended adjacent to a park consisting of several large sports playing fields. They could see streetlights on the far side, so 8th Avenue must pick up again. They crossed the park at a walk. As they approached the street again, Paul caught a glimpse of a gray and tan tail disappearing behind a house.

"I think the coyote is here," Paul said. "Stay close."

They continued down the street, and the coyote slipped out from behind some evergreens ahead of them. It stood and looked at them. Paul stopped, but Amy kept going. He put his arm in front of her.

"Well, child," the coyote said, "you progressed further than I thought you would."

"What is it?" Amy whispered, looking around.

"He's right there," Paul whispered back.

"I don't see anything."

The coyote let out a barking chuckle. "How sweet you look, protecting your little friend. But it is no use. I will have this one, too."

Anger welled up in Paul's chest, burning against the dark touch of the Adversary on his mind. "Liar! You won't have Amy and you don't have Joe. He's in the arms of Jesus and safe. Just as all believers are safe, redeemed."

"You only know what you've been told, or what you read in the Bible," he said with seething scorn. "God hides from his believers. Can't you see? Where is he when you need him? He certainly isn't here now, is he? You are about to fail and I am about to win the whole world, including your dear Amy. And you!"

Paul's confidence wavered.

"You are so close, but this will be as far as you go," the coyote continued. "The police are looking for you, and there are others. I will have you, and her, and the rest of the world soon."

"You will never have me!" Paul said, but his voice shook.

"Don't be too sure," the coyote said and turned, eyes glowing red. He vanished behind the evergreens.

"I heard some kind of weird laughter," Amy said. "Is he still there?"

"No, he left," Paul said. The oily, slimy touch of the Adversary was leaving him. "I think he has some other surprise for us. We know the cops are on our trail, and if the coyote knows where we are, we have to assume the police and anyone else he's sending after us know too."

"They have alleys here," Any said, then pointed up a cross street. "Let's go down the alleys for a bit."

"Good idea."

They walked down the alleys for several blocks. It was dark and difficult to see ahead, and Amy stayed close to Paul. Unfortunately, every other house had a dog inside or outside that started barking as they passed.

"This is only going to attract more attention," Paul said. "Let's move up to 9th Avenue. The dogs are just too focused on the alleys."

After traveling a few blocks more, and seeing glimpses of police cars out on 10th Avenue, Paul had another idea. He got out his map while they were near a street lamp.

"Look," he said. "There are two ways across the river here--the route they think we're taking, along 10th Avenue, and this one, on 1st. We'll have to go through town, but they may not expect that."

"Good, let's go."

Paul put the map away, and they took off. They went a block north, then a block west. They zig-zagged this way until they reached 1st Avenue, then passed a Hardee's, went under an overpass, and came to the bridge across the Missouri River. It was late and little traffic moved on the bridge.

Nothing to do but go for it, Paul thought. Then he saw something he hadn't expected. There was a parallel bridge for pedestrians and bicycles. A sign labeled it "River's Edge Trail."

"That looks like a better way," Paul said, pointing at the smaller bridge. "We'll be harder to spot there. Once we start, we just go until we get across. Maybe we can find a place to hide and rest a bit on the other side. Ready?"

"Yeah, I'm ready."

They moved away from the road and onto the trail bridge. The crossing was uneventful. Walking, they kept a low profile. If anyone saw them from the vehicle bridge, there was no indication.

"I need a restroom," Amy said.

"Me, too. I think we have a solution up ahead," Paul said. There was a KFC, still open, up the road a couple of blocks. The road, now called Central Avenue, was a broad, multi-lane, well-lit street. They trotted along. The less they were exposed on the street, Paul felt, the better their chances.

They made it to the KFC, got inside, used the restrooms, and went to the front to buy something to drink. The counter person looked annoyed.

"Hey! We're just about to close up," he said as Paul and Amy.

"We'll be quick," Paul said. "We'll order drinks and get out of your way."

But when they turned around, two police officers were waiting for them.

"Put the packs and sticks on the ground," one officer said. "We need to see some identification."

His name tag read Jones.

Paul and Amy put down their sticks and packs. Paul pulled out his school ID card, the only thing he had with his photo on it, and handed it to the officer.

"North Carolina?" Jones said. "What are you doing in Montana?"

"How old are you?" the other officer asked. His name tag read Smith.

"Fourteen," Amy and Paul answered together.

"Do your parents know where you are?" Smith asked.

"Our parents are trapped in Charlotte," Paul said. "We aren't able to reach them. They're under the dome."

Jones spoke into the mic on his shoulder.

"We're taking you down to the precinct," he said. "We'll sort out what to do with you there."

Within a few minutes, Paul and Amy were cuffed and put into the back seat of a cruiser, and their packs and staffs were tossed into the trunk.

CHAPTER SIXTEEN

Jail

THE PRECINCT was a cold, institutional place in the main part of Great Falls. *Two steps forward, one step back*, Paul thought as they sat on a couple of chairs waiting for who knew what. At least the cuffs were off now that they were in the precinct. The officers took their packs into another room, emptied them and inspected the contents. After a bit, they came out holding the alien sticks.

"What are these?" Smith asked.

"They are some kind of blaster weapon," Paul said. "But they only work when one of the alien saucers is nearby, far as I can tell."

"What!" Smith said. "Aliens?"

He examined the stick and found the button. He pressed it, but nothing happened.

"Looks like a toy," he said. "I think you're playing games, here, kid."

"No, sir," Paul said. He thought about telling Smith about the attack in Buffalo, Wyoming. Then thought better of it. No sense implicating themselves in all that destruction and loss of life.

"You said your parents are trapped in Charlotte," Jones said as he came out of the other room. "How did that happen?"

"Someone called them and told them we had a relative in the hospital," Amy said. "They went to Charlotte, and then we heard that a dome had come down over the city. No one has been able to enter or leave, and there hasn't been any communication."

"You've heard of the weird things happening around the world, right?" Paul asked.

"You mean like the black fog over Washington, D.C.? Yeah, heard of it," Smith said. "That's not saying I believe it."

"Add Rapid City to that black fog list," Paul said.

"And add St. Louis as the city that just stopped," Amy added.

The officers stood and studied the kids for a bit.

"Okay," Smith said. "We can't do anything with you tonight. We're going to put you in cells for the evening and have the county social worker come in and sort out what to do in the morning."

"How can you do that?" Paul asked. "We haven't done anything wrong."

"Not that we know of," Jones said. "But we do have a citizen complaint. And you are juveniles with no parental supervision."

Citizen complaint, Paul thought. Sherman.

The cold sterility of the environment extended to the cells. A stainless steel commode, a small stainless steel sink, a bed with a sheet and a blanket, and a bare concrete floor were the accommodations. Amy was put in one cell, Paul in another. They were told to keep quiet and go to sleep, and there would be breakfast in the morning. At least the cells were clean.

#

Morning brought a fresh bustle of activity. Breakfast came around. Oatmeal, a small carton of milk, and a small bottle of orange juice. Eventually, the county social worker came and got the two of them into an interview room with a table and three chairs.

"I'm Marian," she said, setting her legal pad down on the table. "I'll be handling your case." She made some notes on the pad.

"What case?" Paul asked.

"The case of what to do with you. It seems you're without adult supervision and may be involved in some mischief. We cannot contact your parents."

"We know where our parents are," Amy said. "They are in Charlotte."

"Yes, but we cannot contact them." Marian made some additional notes on the pad.

"No one can contact anyone in Charlotte," Paul said.

"Don't get smart with me, young man," she glanced at her notes. "Mr. Paul Shannon. Our concern is getting you into a stable home environment and under adult supervision." She wrote on the pad.

Amy and Paul looked at each other, eyebrows raised.

"I have something to do in Choteau," Paul said. "I have to do this to free our parents and correct some other things."

"What do you have to do?" More notes appeared on the pad.

"I don't know yet. I just know I have to get to Choteau." Marian wrote the name of the town on the pad and then some additional notes.

"Well, that is a pretty far stretch, Mr. Shannon!" Marian said, looking down her nose at him. "Choteau is a little town in the middle of nowhere. What could possibly be there that you would have to find or do? And what would it possibly have to do with Charlotte, North Carolina?"

"I don't know, ma'am," Paul said. He could tell she wouldn't take the whole story well, so he just kept it as simple as possible. "I just know I'm supposed to go there."

Marian wrote some more notes. "Looks like a psychological assessment is in order for the two of you. For now, though, we have a place for you and we're going to transport you there. In a few days, we'll have you evaluated by our psychologist. When your parents can be contacted, we will arrange your transportation back to North Carolina."

Marian reached down to pick up her legal pad and her long sleeve slid up just a bit, exposing her left wrist. Amy's eyebrows raised and she looked pointedly at Paul.

"You will be escorted to the room where your personal belongings are," Marian said, standing. "You can repack your things, then we will take you to your placement."

Two police officers they hadn't seen before came into the room when Marian waved for them. Paul and Amy followed them to the room where their packs had been examined. Everything was there, including the alien sticks. Paul figured the officers thought they were toys and didn't confiscate them. Even their staffs were there, scarred and beat up as they were.

He and Amy packed up their clothing and supplies. When they shouldered their packs and stood with their staffs, holding them like walking sticks, they were led out of the precinct to a car where Marian was waiting. She opened the back door to the sedan and the officers escorting Amy and Paul pushed them in. Marian closed the door. The first thing Paul and Amy noticed was that they couldn't open the car doors from the inside and there was a barrier between the front and back seat.

"Marian belongs to the Adversary," Amy whispered while Marian walked around to the driver's side of the car. "Left wrist. Pitchfork."

Paul just nodded. He'd seen, too. Marian probably knew more about his mission than she'd admitted.

Marian got in and started the car.

In the silence Paul took stock of their situation. Being locked inside a car driven by one of the agents of the Adversary was definitely a strike against them. On the plus side, he and Amy had all their belongings, including the sticks and staffs. And since he now knew that Marian belonged to the Adversary, he started thinking about how they might break away.

He paid attention to where they went. Marian drove across the bridge and down Central Avenue, then over I-15. She then turned off Central Avenue and onto an unpaved, narrow street several intersections away from the interstate. Piles of bricks and abandoned vehicles mixed with the widely spaced houses and manufactured homes that populated this neighborhood. The odd piece of heavy equipment filled Paul's view, and there were recreational vehicles parked in yards.

Marian pulled up behind an RV in front of a long, low house. He didn't see anyone out around the house or in the neighborhood.

Marian got out and opened the door on Amy's side.

"Get out, now!" she demanded.

They did, taking their time. Eventually, they stood next to the car, packs shouldered and holding their staffs.

"You won't need walking sticks inside. Just toss them over the fence there," she said and pointed to a chain link fence.

Paul picked up the staff as though he was going to throw it, then thrust at Marian's midsection. Amy, quick on the uptake, spun her staff and whacked Marian on the side of her head as she bent over from Paul's thrust. Down she went like a sack of potatoes.

Paul bent down to check her, putting his hand on her neck.

"She's not dead," he said, hoping he knew what he was talking about. He grabbed her keys out of her hand and got up. He considered taking the car, but discarded that thought right away. He'd probably get them both killed trying to drive. He looked around to see if they had attracted any attention.

"Let's get her in back," he said. He opened the back door of the car and the two lifted Marian into the back seat. Amy closed the door with a satisfied grin, leaving Marian locked in from the outside.

"That should hold her for a while," she said as they shouldered their gear and left.

Paul led the way back to Central Avenue and then turned toward the interstate. When they passed a broad, open field, Paul threw Marian's keys as far as he could into the tall grass.

"When she wakes up, it'll be a while before she can come after us," he said.

"I just hope we get a ride right away," Amy said. "I want to get to Choteau and get this done."

They got over the freeway and down the northbound ramp. They had to walk beyond the guardrails at the top of the ramp before there was room to safely stand on the shoulder and hitchhike.

"If the cops think Marian has us locked up," Paul said, "they shouldn't be looking for us. We should at least be able to get out of this area."

"We need to keep an eye out for those little tattoos, too," Amy said. "I bet Sherman had one."

"He may have." Paul got the map out of the pack. "It's only about ten miles until we get off the freeway and go down US 89."

He shoved the map back in his pack and stood with his thumb out. After a few minutes, a pickup pulled over.

"We're heading for Choteau," Paul said through the passenger window.

"I'm heading for Shelby, but I can drop you at the interchange," the driver said.

"That works!"

"Great. Put your stuff in the back and climb in."

Paul did the introductions once they were moving. The driver, Jerry, was a student at University of Great Falls. He said he was studying to be a teacher. Paul and Amy chatted with him about school and what they wanted to study when they got to college, and the trip was over after about ten minutes.

Jerry pulled over to the shoulder and let them off at the ramp.

"Good luck, you two!" he said and waited for them to get their gear from the back.

"Thanks," Paul said and patted the side of the truck. Jerry took off. They walked up the ramp and around over the freeway.

The small town of Vaughn straddled US 89. They walked through, stopping for some portable food, snacks, and drinks at a gas station. Further on, they set their packs down on the side of the road on the west side of the little town.

"We only have about forty miles to go," Paul said. "We're so close. I just hope we don't have to walk the rest of the way."

"Getting low on cash, too," Amy said. "How much you got left?"

"About fifty bucks," he said. "You?"

"Forty-five. When you consider how far we've come, we did pretty good."

"Have you had any ideas on what we might find in Choteau?"

"None," she said. "You get any clues from the coyote or Gabriel?"

"No."

"We didn't get a chance to talk about what the coyote said last time," Amy said.

A chill pass through Paul. "I know."

Amy waited. "Well, what did he say?"

"He said he would have me . . . and you."

Amy stood directly in front of him, forcing him to look at her. "Paul, you know that's not true."

"I know." He did know, and he felt almost embarrassed that the coyote's words bothered him so much--bothered him still, to tell the truth. His faith ought to be stronger. "But when he's actually talking to you, it's hard to believe. He also said he had the police and others working to get us, and that turned out to be true. I wonder . . . "

"What?"

"Well, doesn't it seem like we got away awfully easy from Marian and the police? They didn't seem to have any good info on us. They should have known about the alien sticks. If any information flows from the Adversary's minions, they should have known we were dangerous with the staffs. Something just isn't adding up."

"Like, it just seems like he's throwing people and things in front of us hoping one of them will get lucky?"

"Or," Paul said, stretching with his arms over his head, "he's trying to get us thinking that. And he has something really nasty waiting down the road."

"Can I make a suggestion?" Amy asked, sniffing the air.

"Sure." He looked at her. He realized that he had come to depend on her cool head and judgment. He'd always admired Amy's intelligence and over the last few days he'd learned to value her and her contribution to their mission more than ever. Even now, when things seem so bleak and they were running low on options and reserves, he could tell by the serious look on her face that she was about to impart some rare insight.

"The breeze is blowing from the west. We're downwind of a feed lot. I think we should move to the other side of the feed lot or I'm going to lose what little food I just ate."

Paul laughed out loud.

"What? What's so funny?"

"Nothing. Nothing. You're right. Let's go."

CHAPTER SEVENTEEN

Aliens Again

THEY WALKED about a mile. The air was much fresher, but the road was pretty empty. The few vehicles that did drive by seemed to be local. In any case, no one stopped. Trees grew thinly around ponds, small oxbow lakes, and the river to the south. And there were a few houses further down the road. To the north, the land just went to the horizon in a flat, empty stretch.

The day was fading and Paul and Amy just walked along the road. It was a way to kill time while trying to get a ride. Paul thought they would want to find a well-lit spot when it got dark. They had just passed a small house along the right side and Paul could see a line of trees ahead.

"This is a nice, clear spot," he said. "The yard light should give us a little illumination."

"I'm not feeling the love here," Amy said. "I want a ride!"

Paul laughed and high-fived Amy. "I'd like a ride, too!"

He reached up to pull his pack off his shoulder. Something vibrated inside. He set the pack down and opened it up.

The alien stick was shaking and humming. A sick feeling settled in the pit of his stomach. The memory of Joe's death and his inability to do anything about it came back. Not aliens, again, he thought as he pulled the stick from his pack and looked around. The deaths and burning buildings in Buffalo colored his vision as he scanned the fields and trees.

"Amy, get your stick out," Paul said. "We may have company."

Nothing moved in the open fields on the north or south.

Then a large shadow caught Paul's eye beyond the trees ahead. It moved.

"Over there," he said, pointing. "Take the packs into the ditch here. I'm going to the other side. Stay down, but keep watching. The sticks are active, so there must be a saucer nearby. I think it's behind the trees."

"If the saucer shows itself, we should take it out," Amy said. "Then we can deal with the aliens with the staffs."

"Never mind that now! Just get in the ditch and stay there. Move along the road if you need to, but it's your best cover."

Amy cringed at the sharp tone from Paul but started to move. Paul saw and immediately felt pangs of guilt for speaking that way to her. His emotions churned inside. He couldn't tell if he was concerned for Amy's safety, upset about Joe, or just generally angry at aliens. Maybe it was all the above. In any case, he knew he couldn't lose Amy, too.

"Go," he said.

The movement Paul had seen turned out to be about two dozen aliens that must have unloaded from a saucer behind the trees. With this many aliens, there might actually be two saucers, or even three.

After a few minutes trotting in formation out in the open, the aliens burned down a small business on the south side of the road. Flames billowed up, then a propane tank and a car exploded in huge fireballs. The aliens continued at a trot along the middle of the road toward Paul and Amy. Anger grew inside him again. *Vengeance is the Lord's*, he thought, *not mine.*

Paul looked around in the dimming light. A frontage road crossed the main highway just ahead. The slope on their side would provide good cover from the approaching aliens.

"Amy," he said, waving to get her attention. "Move up to the crossroad. It's better cover."

Paul moved up on his side. The access slope provided an excellent place to ambush the aliens, he thought. The aliens trotted in two files on each side of the highway. A couple--Paul figured they were leaders or sergeants--in the middle of the road ran along with the troops. He marked those as the first targets.

Could they see him or Amy? Or were they just charging ahead and taking on targets of opportunity? He double-checked the position of the trigger button on his stick and brought it up as the aliens got close enough to what he thought of as the stick's range.

The beam from his stick shot out, vaporizing the first leader and two aliens behind him. Amy fired and burned down four in a row on her side of the road. Paul shifted to the column on his side and held the button until the buzzing and warmth from the stick were almost unbearable. He released the button and peered through the smoke to see that there were only eight aliens left, plus one of the leaders. Amy hit them with bursts and burned them down quickly. Paul fired a few more times, and there were no more aliens.

But there were probably two, maybe three saucers on the other side of those trees. He couldn't see any more movement from the trees yet.

"You okay, Amy?" he asked.

"Yes," she said. "It was almost too easy, though."

Paul looked around, checking behind them to make sure something wasn't coming up while the aliens kept them busy. Something had come up. A car rolled to a stop nearby and the dark-haired, heavyset driver got out.

"What in the heck is going on here?" he asked, looking at the smoking ruins of aliens bathed in his headlights. "You guys shooting off fireworks?"

"Aliens," Paul said, waving the smoke from the burnt little green men away from his face.

"You have got to be kidding me," he said. Paul noted his bushy dark hair and heavy mustache.

"Nope," Paul said, climbing out of the ditch and heading back to the packs. When he reached the man's car, he said, "There are a couple of saucers behind those trees, up there."

Amy came over and retrieved her pack and staff from Paul.

"Second time we've had to fight them," she said.

"What are those?" the man asked, pointing to the sticks.

"Blasters," Paul said, "I think." He looked at the car, then at the tree line. "Think you can give us a lift close to those trees?"

"Why?"

"Well, we still have to take out the saucers, the spaceships," Amy said. "It's a long walk and I'm tired."

"You're just a couple of kids," he said. "What makes you think you can take out some spaceships?"

"Come along and find out," Paul said. He opened the back door and looked at the man.

He looked at Amy and Paul, then shrugged. "Aliens. Sure, why not? That's as good an explanation as any for the world going to pot and the stuff that's been going on the last week or so. Okay, get in."

"Just go slow, don't close your doors. If anything starts glowing by the trees, stop, get out, and run," Paul said.

Sal--short for Salvatore, he said--drove slowly, winding through the still-smoking remains on the road. After a couple of minutes, they were adjacent to the remains of the small business.

"What happened here?" Sal asked.

"The aliens destroyed it," Amy said. "They seem to just blast anything along their path. That's why you run if the ships come up. They blast everything in sight, too."

They got close to the tree line and Paul asked Sal to stop.

"We should go on foot here," he said. "It might save your car."

Paul led them to the trees. The fences around the fields here were all beaten down. Air displacement from the landing saucers, maybe? Paul thought. The saucers didn't look big enough to cause this much knockdown, but there could be strange physics involved.

Paul, Amy, and Sal moved carefully over the fence wires and posts and into the trees. From here they could see a tree-lined lane that led to the smoking ruin of a house on the north side of the road. They moved across the lane and stopped on the other side. Through the trees they could see three saucers sitting in the large field beyond.

"They're just sitting there," Amy said, "with their ramps down."

"Suppose any aliens are still on board? Or are they empty?" Paul said.

Sal just stood staring with his jaw hanging loose.

"I don't see anyone moving around," Amy said. "I want to get a look inside one of those."

"Really?" Sal said.

"Yeah, really," Amy said.

"Well, let's keep alert," Paul said, and indicated the nearest saucer. "Let's try that one. Burn any aliens you see."

They moved carefully across the field and started up the ramp to the first saucer. Paul stopped when his head cleared the saucer floor and he could see inside.

"No one around," he whispered. He moved up more and kept looking around. The inside perimeter was lined with what looked like harnesses. They were about the right size to strap in the alien troops. What looked like a console was across from the end of the ramp, and there was a window or viewscreen on that side. He stepped into the craft.

"There's nowhere to hide in here," Paul said. "Come on up."

Amy and Sal followed as Paul moved to the console. Through the window he could see the other two saucers as clearly as if it were daylight. "Pretty cool," he said, pointing.

Amy poked around the harnesses. Sal just stood in the middle in awe.

"They don't go far with these," Amy said, twirling her arm around to indicate the saucer. "There isn't anywhere to sleep, eat, or anything."

"Do you think these are just shuttles or troop transports?" Paul asked.

"Yeah, I bet there's a mothership or some kind of huge carrier in orbit," Amy said.

Paul examined the console. There was a circle in the center, and a button next to it, similar to the button on his stick. When he touched the circle, a green "x" appeared in the window. When he moved his finger around on the circle, the "x" moved around in the window. He centered the "x" on the next saucer; the "x" turned red. Curious, Paul then pressed the button on the console.

A beam shot out of their craft and hit the next one. After a moment, the other craft glowed, then disappeared. He repeated the process on the third saucer.

"I wonder if we're upsetting the mother ship," Paul said, secretly hoping he was doing just that.

"Wow," Sal said. "Do you think you can fly this thing?"

"I'm not even going to try," Paul said. "These guys are not geniuses when it comes to ground combat, but I would not want to try dogfighting one of these against one of their pilots. That would be a quick route to Heaven."

"This ship could get us to Choteau in a snap," Amy said.

"If we don't crash and die first," Paul said.

"Well, let's not risk that," Sal said. "You're going to Choteau?"

"Yeah," Paul said.

"I was heading to Freezeout Lake to do some fishing. I can take you that far."

"That would be very appreciated," Paul said heading down the ramp. "Let's get out of this thing and burn it away."

"Sal, you could bring the car closer while Paul and I dispose of this saucer," Amy said, following Paul.

"Good idea." Sal hustled down the ramp and went to his car.

Paul and Amy walked to the road, separated a bit, then blasted the saucer until it popped out of existence. The sticks, of course, went dead.

"These sticks are pretty handy," Paul said. "If they send any more saucers down, the sticks make a good early warning."

Paul barely made out her nod in the darkness.

"Paul," Amy said pointing to the downed fences, "all these fences are knocked down. Kinda like something came through and rolled over them. Look, all down the tree line, across the road."

"Yeah, I noticed that earlier and thought it might be air displacement or some other effect of the saucers. But this is too big an area for that. And it's all going in one direction, not in a circle."

"We didn't see anything like this in Buffalo," she added. "Is it something else, something new, or is it even connected with the aliens?"

Sal drove up with the car.

"We'll keep an eye out," Paul said, and got in.

They'd driven less than a mile when Paul saw another large shadow in another tree line.

"Stop here for a minute, Sal." He got out and waved Amy out. "I think we're about to find what's mashing down the fences."

He moved into the trees, keeping his staff ready. Amy paralleled him, her own staff ready. They approached a large shadow on the other side of the trees.

As they got closer, Paul heard voices. Near the large shadow, there were two small figures speaking and waving their arms around. He couldn't make sense of what was being said, but he could identify the small, green creatures.

"Aliens," Amy whispered.

"I think that big shadow is what's been tearing down the fences," he whispered back. "You come around that way, I'll go here. Let's see if we can get anything from these guys."

They crept around and approached from behind the aliens. Paul's feet crunched in the dry stubble and the aliens stopped talking and spun around.

Paul had his staff pointed directly at the chest of one of the aliens. Amy covered the other.

"Where do you come from?" Paul asked, not really expecting a response he could understand.

One alien let out a scream and made a wild attack at Amy. It went down like a wet rag under the spinning defense of her staff.

"If you know our language, talk now!" Paul said.

His huge eyes even wider, the second alien looked at them, then at his friend lying in a heap on the ground. He shook himself, then looked smug. He waved his hand at Paul and Amy as though they meant little to him.

"Ve keel you! Ve take thees place for us. You . . . " he waved at them again, "You no more."

"Really?" Paul said. We're being invaded by barely competent aliens, Paul thought, and they don't think we'll be a problem for them.

"You came to kill us?" Amy asked. "And you want to take our planet?"

"Yessssss," it said, nodding its ovoid head. "You no more."

"Well, there's a whole lot more of us that just the two of us," Paul said. He wave his alien stick. "We know how to use your weapons, too."

The alien looked stricken, then unsure.

"So what were you doing with this?" Paul pointed at the large machine.

"Ve prepare lantink place and place for varriors."

"Your machine is broken," Paul said, guessing that it took power from the saucers, like the sticks did. "So what happens now?"

"Vait," it said. "No power."

That verified Paul's suspicion.

"Wait? How long? How do you tell them your troops were killed?" he asked.

The alien shook its head and gave a very human-like shrug. "No talk." It waved its hand from its mouth to the night sky, then sat down on the ground and put its head on its knees.

Paul relaxed. He got a better look at the big shadow. It resembled a large steam roller but had some other appendages. A ladder provided a way up to a small console on top.

"I don't know what these guys have to do with the coyote," Amy said, looking up from the unconscious alien. "They don't seem to fit in the scheme. They don't have any marks I can see."

"I wonder if this is just coincidental, or if they're just part of the twisted reality we live in now," Paul said, swinging his staff and keeping an eye on the aliens.

"My money's on the twisted reality," Amy said. "This is pretty twisted."

Paul looked at the aliens. The one Amy had laid low was still out. The other seemed pretty defeated. Neither was armed.

"Hey," Paul said, poking his alien with his staff. It cringed back and held up its hands defensively. "Your boss up there?" He pointed to the sky.

"Yesssss."

"You tell them, go home or we kill them!" Paul said and pulled the alien stick out of his belt. He displayed it to the cringing alien. It raised his hands defensively. "You tell them I said, 'Go home.'"

CHAPTER EIGHTEEN

Forest

PAUL WASN'T going to kill the two unarmed aliens. That just didn't sit right with him. Still, they presented a danger to their backs, as well as the rest of the planet. If he stayed and waited for the mothership or more saucers, he may be there a while, or get caught up in something more than he could handle.

He looked at the still-conscious alien as he prepared to leave. The alien nodded. Paul felt certain that his message would be transmitted. Just what the aliens would do about it, though, was another thing.

They left the two little aliens alone and got back in the car. Paul and Amy gave Sal the story of their trip as they drove into the night.

"The coyote said he had more to meet us," Paul said. "If the aliens aren't his direct allies or under his control, we may still have more to face."

"That whole thing in Great Falls can't be the best he could do," Amy said. "That was lame. I bet it was designed to just delay us."

They had been driving for about ten minutes and Paul sat forward looking at the road. "Sal, when was the last time another car came the other way?"

"I haven't seen anything come this way since I met you guys," he said. "Usually there are grain trucks coming and going from the grain bins in Fairfield. Nothing tonight."

"Is Fairfield close?"

"Yeah, just a mile or so now."

Even a small town should have some lights. Paul scanned the dark for signs of the town. No lights, not even farm yard lights.

"Sal," he said, "slow down. Something is up."

Sal did as Paul asked. The road curved to the right, heading almost directly north. The terrain ahead was dark and ominous. Sal brought the car to a stop. The headlights pierced the darkness ahead to where the highway abruptly ended.

"That's never been there before," Sal said.

The asphalt quit, giving way to grass-covered ground with a packed dirt trail about thirty feet in front of them. About another twenty yards farther, they could dimly see the beginnings of a thick forest. To the left and right, the huge trees marched as far as they could see in the starlit dark.

They all got out and Paul and Amy approached the forest. Sal stayed by the car. The well-worn trail led from the road into the forest. It was a narrow track. They could see nothing beyond the entry of the trail into the trees.

Paul walked a way to the right to see if there were any other trails. Amy did the same to the left. They shook their heads as they returned a few minutes later.

To the east, the first glow of predawn was lightening the night sky.

"We have to go through," Paul said. "Not right now, though."

"Could we have a rest in your car until the sun comes up, Sal?" Amy asked when they got back to the car. "I'm pretty tired. We could get a few hours' nap before it's light enough to continue."

"Sure," Sal said. "I planned to start fishing at dawn, but it doesn't look like I'll be getting to Freezeout."

Paul watched from the car as the predawn turned to sunrise and the immense forest was slowly revealed. It stretched in front of them and as far as he could see to either side. Huge ancient-looking trees, both evergreen and deciduous, towered higher than he had ever seen, creating a dense canopy. He expected that even with full daylight, it would be very dark on the trail. He was tired, too, and he dozed.

#

Paul woke with a start. Amy shook him through the back window. It was full daylight and she was standing outside the car with her pack on and her staff in hand.

"Where'd you go?" Paul asked.

All he got from Amy in answer was a level gaze.

"Oh," he said, getting out of the car. He looked around. No other cars in the area, and the few farmhouses he could see from here looked abandoned.

Sal sat in the driver's seat, looking at the forest.

"You might as well go home, Sal," Paul said after coming around to his side of the car. "I bet this'll stay until we complete our mission."

"Probably," he agreed. "You guys have food and water?"

"Yeah," Paul said. "Not sure how long they'll last."

"Well, let's have a little breakfast," Sal said. He got out of the car, opened the trunk, and pulled out a cooler. "I brought this for some breakfast before fishing. We can make a good meal here before you go."

He opened the cooler. Inside were a dozen eggs, bacon, ham, bread, and all the condiments.

Amy let out a sigh of happiness. "Look, Paul! Ingredients!"

Paul nodded. He knew what she meant. After all these days on the road, he was sick of fast food, and they had little left in their packs that was edible. Home-cooked meals were a cause for celebration.

In this case, not exactly home-cooked, but close enough. Sal lifted out another box that he expanded up to a small gas grill. After connecting a bottle of gas to it, he fired it up and started cooking.

Paul and Amy dug into the thick breakfast sandwiches Sal made and washed them down with cold water. As the two cleaned up from breakfast and readied their packs, Sal packed his cooler and grill back in the trunk. Then he dug through a bag and got a palm-sized metal capsule.

He tossed Paul the capsule. "You probably don't have matches, do you? Those are waterproof matches. You'll probably need them."

"Thanks!" Paul said. "I hadn't thought of that."

"You know how to make a fire?"

"If he doesn't," Amy said, "I do."

Paul then gave Amy the capsule of matches.

"How about a knife?"

"Uh, no," Paul said.

Sal reached in his bag again. He brought out a small folding two-blade pocket knife. He handed it to Paul. One blade was longer and the other short. On the side of the brown bone handle was a shiny metal badge that said, "Old Timer."

"Take good care of that," he said. "My grandpa gave me that knife when I was twelve."

"I will," Paul said. He shouldered his pack and placed the knife in his jeans pocket. "Thanks, Sal. You've been a great help."

"I know there's a lot more to what you're doing than I realize," he said. "I hope whatever is going on, you two kids will fix it."

He shook hands with Paul and Amy, closed up the trunk, got in the car, and drove off. Amy and Paul waved as Sal's car headed back toward Vaughn. Then they turned and looked at the forest.

"All we can do now is try to get through," Paul said.

"I'm going to be praying with every step," Amy said.

They walked to the edge, then entered the forest. Behind them the path was bare hard-packed dirt, but inside the forest it was cushioned with old needles and leaves. The forest canopy shut out most of the light, darkening the trail, which then wound around trees and undergrowth, making it doubly difficult to see very far ahead.

Paul listened as they walked, trying to identify any sounds that came from the forest. Chirps and twits were probably from squirrels and birds. There were other sounds, like that of a falling branch, or something scooting around in the leaves and needles off the trail.

After about an hour, they paused to drink from one of their bottles. Paul estimated they had covered about two miles, maybe more. With the winding trail, he guessed, they would be lucky if they got more than a mile, as the crow flies.

"I think it'll take a couple of days to get to Choteau at this rate," he told Amy. He calculated Choteau was about eighteen miles from where the forest had begun before they'd started.

They walked for about another hour. The trail seemed to wind around less, and they came to a crossroads. There were three options: left, right and straight ahead--which didn't stay straight ahead for long. Paul and Amy stood while Paul studied the crossing.

"Three choices," Paul said. "Of course, a fourth would be to just turn around and go back the way we came."

"Don't you do that, Paul," Amy said. "Don't start that negative thinking. We can do this."

"I know, I know," he said, shifting his pack on his shoulders.

"Well, the obvious choice is to take that path," Amy said, pointing to the straight ahead option.

"Yeah, obvious," he said. "So that makes me suspicious."

Paul broke a piece off a dead branch near the trail, broke that in half, and handed one piece to Amy.

"Okay, stay here," he said. "I'm going to mark the straight-ahead trail."

He crossed the trail intersection, looked back to ake sure Amy was still there, then pushed his broken stick into the soil at the side of the trail. It went in about three inches, and Paul thought that would be good. He indicated to Amy to mark the trail on her side.

"We'll go this way for a bit. If it turns out to be good, we don't have to come back. If we do have to come back, we have it marked. We can choose another way then."

"Getting a little paranoid?" she asked as she joined him.

"Not without good reason," he replied.

CHAPTER NINETEEN

Gingerbread

THE TRAIL turned and twisted but seemed to favor left. It led down a draw and around a small hill. As they came around the hill, Paul saw a clearing with a small cottage in the middle. Light filtered down through the thinner canopy over the clearing, revealing some weird-looking plants and flowers around the cottage.

As they got closer, he noticed some of the plants had blossoms that looked like, well, cupcakes. The air was filled with a sweet, seductive aroma. The good breakfast they'd had with Sal was no more than a memory now, and Paul realized he was famished.

Before Paul could stop her, Amy hurried to the house, plucked off one of the cupcake flowers and took a bite. She shoved the rest into her mouth and gobbled it down. He resisted the urge to do the same.

"Oh, Paul, you should try these!" she said through a mouthful of cupcake.

Paul's internal alarm bells rang. He grabbed Amy's arm. "Don't eat any more yet."

"But, look, there are lemonade fruits!"

She was struggling to get away, and Paul tried not to hurt her as he held her in his arms. "Hold on," he said. "Let's check this out a little better."

Paul looked behind them and knew they were in some kind of trap. There were six trails entering the clearing, and he couldn't tell which was the one that brought them here. *We're in trouble now,* he thought.

His own hunger was getting stronger by the second. His grasp on

Amy slackened just a little. She shook herself loose from Paul's grasp and grabbed a lemonade fruit. She wrapped her lips around the stem and sucked out the lemonade. Then she walked over to the cottage and put her hands on some of the fancy trim on the side. A piece broke off at her touch and she immediately put it in her mouth.

"Gingerbread, Paul!" she said. He caught up to her, his mouth open to protest, but before he could speak she shoved a chunk of the gingerbread into his mouth.

He stopped in his tracks as the spicy sweetness melted in his mouth, capturing his senses. He chewed and swallowed, then found a lemonade fruit and drank. The citrusy tartness was a perfect follow-up to the gingerbread's dark, rich flavor. While still savoring the lemonade fruit, he saw a plant that had blossoms made of doughnuts, covered in chocolate and sprinkles.

"How do they do that?" he said, then shoved one into his mouth. It tasted even better than it looked.

"How do who do what?" Amy replied.

He looked at Amy. Maybe it was the sugar rush, or a combination of fatigue and nervous strain, but somehow Amy's question hit him as the funniest thing anyone ever said, ever.

Paul laughed. Amy laughed. She had a huge grin on her face and the area around her mouth was smeared with sugary frosting. After everything they'd been through, Paul felt euphoric. He couldn't stop laughing. He laughed harder and harder.

Then everything went black.

#

He was warm, but not comfortable. His hands were tied. He could move them a little, and he felt other hands. He opened his eyes and craned his neck. Amy was there, her hands tied to the same post his hands were tied to. She was still sleeping. The sugary frosting he remembered smeared on her face was gone.

They were in a room with a huge stove at one end. A hunched old woman, as far as Paul could guess, stoked the fire in the stove. On a large woodblock table next to the stove she had vegetables and fruits laid out for chopping and a huge roasting pan nearby. Across the room was another table with a plate, knife, fork, spoon, and huge napkin. Just one place setting.

The old woman turned to work on her vegetables and fruits. She wore a kerchief around her hair and had a long, hooked nose. She wiped her hands on her dirty apron, then picked up a large knife and started chopping and tossing things into the roasting pan.

Paul tried to work at the ropes around his wrists but couldn't get any leverage. The pocket knife was, well, in his pocket, and that was out of reach. He tried to reach Amy's ropes but wasn't able to get to the knots. *This is straight out of Hansel and Gretel,* he thought. That made a strange kind of sense, though.

He saw their packs over near the door, with the staffs leaning against the wall nearby.

The old woman turned his direction. "Ah, you're awake," she said. She had a sharp, raspy voice. A perfect fit for her crone-like appearance. Then she grunted and turned back to her work.

"What's for dinner?" Paul asked, as if he didn't know.

"You, first," the old woman said, then turned toward him again and cackled a nasty-sounding laugh. "You first, then your little sweetie."

She tottered over to him and pinched his arm and poked his chest. Her fingers were twisted and the joints knobby.

"How long has it been since you roasted a fine young boy?" Paul asked as she tottered back to the chopping block.

"Oh, too long, too long, indeed," she said, turning back to her chopping. "I'm looking forward to it, though."

"Well, we're a little tough and hard to chew. Fine young girls are much more tender and juicy."

"What would you know about it?" The old woman tossed a bunch of chopped vegetables into the roaster and shook her head.

"Well, I was going to roast and eat her myself," Paul said, nodding to the still-sleeping Amy. "I was looking for a good place to set up. And I brought some special spices and herbs. There is nothing like fine young girl, roasted slowly and treated with my special herbs and spices."

It was a long shot, Paul knew, but characters in fairy tales were often amazingly gullible. He waited and prayed.

The old woman hobbled over to Paul and looked at him squarely from her hunched position. She glanced at Amy, then back at Paul.

"You've had fine young girl before?"

"Oh, yes, many times. It's my specialty!"

She wiped her hands on her dirty apron again and smacked her lips. She dragged her sleeve across her mouth to wipe away drool. "What are these herbs and spices?" she asked.

"Oh, those are my secret. I'm the only one who knows how to use them properly."

"Really?" The old woman peered at him again, this time with one eye closed. "Oh, you're just lying, trying to fool an old woman." She turned away and went back to chopping.

"I tell you what," Paul said. "I'll show you how to make the best roast of fine young girl, and show you how to use the herbs and spices. After we eat, you can cook me next."

She glanced at Paul, then turned back to her table, mumbling to herself.

"Just think about how much more plump and flavorful I'll be after we have the fine young girl!"

The old woman chopped up some fruit that looked like apples and tossed that into the roaster. She continued to mumble, glancing at Paul a few times. She reached in and arranged the chopped vegetables and fruit in the roaster, then wiped her hands again and turned toward him. The apron was getting pretty filthy.

"How are you going to show me?" she demanded of Paul.

"I'll get the herbs and spices I have hidden in my pack. Then I'll show you how it all works."

"I'll have to let you loose," she said. "You're just trying to get loose to trick this old woman."

"I'm not trying to trick you. You've clearly got me beat, and I could never hope to slip free from a powerful enchantress such as yourself. Everyone has to die sometime, and it looks like this is my time. If I can have one good last meal, I'll die happy, which is a lot more than most people can say.   And nothing is better than fine young girl. I can't get to the wonderful herbs and spices I have hidden in my pack if I'm all tied up here."

She turned away again. At the stove, she opened the big oven briefly, checking the temperature. Then she turned back. She looked longingly at Amy, licking her lips. A gap-toothed grin appeared on her face for a moment. Then she got serious again.

"I will untie you long enough to get the herbs and spices and prepare the fine young girl. As soon as she is roasting, I will tie you back up. I'll feed you with your hands tied."

"That would be just fine," Paul said, a glimmer of hope in his heart.

"Just remember, I have a big knife and can chop you up very quickly," she said. She picked up her big chopping knife and shook it at him. She came over, and with a couple quick flicks of the big knife, Paul's hands were loose. "Your pack is over by the door."

Paul got up, stretched and walked over to his pack, rubbing his wrists. The staffs were also leaning against the wall next to the packs. He made a big show of opening his pack and digging through it.

"You know," he said digging deep in to the pack, "I think your stove needs to be hotter. Fine young girls should be roasted at a higher temperature."

"Are you sure?"

"Absolutely," he said.

The old woman threw a few more pieces of wood into the firebox.

"Ah, here they are," Paul said, watching the old woman out of the corner of his eye. "Why don't you check the oven just to be sure? Then we can prepare the fine young girl!"

The old woman tottered to the oven and opened the large door.

Paul grabbed a staff, swung around, and hit the old woman squarely in the behind, shoving her head first into the oven. She let out a terrible scream.

Still using his staff, Paul jammed the old witch into the oven and quickly slam its door closed. He then shoved the chair from the dining table against the oven door and propped it to keep it closed. The old witch screamed and shouted in the flames as she kicked and banged against the door, then went silent.

Paul pulled out the Old Timer and went over to cut the bonds from Amy's hands.

As she started to rouse, the house and all the strange plants in the clearing faded away. The whole thing must have been an incredibly detailed illusion, complete with flavors and scents, and now with the old woman gone, so was the illusion. By the time Amy was awake, the house site was just a plain, small clearing.

"What happened?" Amy asked.

"We were almost turned into a meal," Paul said. He looked around the clearing. There was only one trail leading in, none leading out. It was a dead end.

"Let's go back to where we marked the trail," he said. "We'll try another one."

He told her the whole story on the way back.

"You were going to show her how to cook me?" Amy asked. "Really?"

"Not really, it was just a ruse to get her to cut me loose. Honest. I remember my Grimm's Tales."

"You wouldn't really cook me, would you?"

"No." He didn't look at her and tried to keep his face serious. She punched him in the shoulder.

"So this old woman, she was a witch?"

"Evidently. Once she was gone, so was her power or illusion. The whole trap just vanished."

"You really cooked her goose," Amy said and started laughing.

"Hey, don't start with the sugar hysteria again. I can't take any more of that."

"Well, I wasn't as bad as you. You were laughing like a hyena."

"What? That's a lie. You were the worst by far. I'm never letting you near sugar again."

They had just survived a kidnapping attempt by a deranged cannibal with magical abilities, Paul had defeated her by shoving her into a hot stove, and now they couldn't stop joking about the whole thing. Travel, Paul thought, certainly was broadening.

CHAPTER TWENTY
Goblins

BACK AT the trail crossing they were faced with two choices. They couldn't see far enough down either trail to get an idea of where they might lead.

"I'd say toss a coin," Paul said, crouching down and examining the tracks they'd left from before. "This last trail was a trap. It could have led to a pretty nasty end for both of us. These other two could be as bad or worse."

Amy looked at the trails a moment, then pointed to the one on their right.

"Let's go down that one next," she said.

Paul broke off a stick from a dead branch and gave it to Amy.

"Go mark it," he said.

She went to the trail on the right and shoved the stick into the soil, as Paul had done before. When she stood, he looked around at the other trails, then stood and crossed the intersection to join Amy. There was no guarantee that something wouldn't change, Paul knew, but not marking the trails just didn't seem prudent.

This trail kept going in the relative direction for a while, then started trending to the right. It was easy going, if winding and slow. They crossed a few streams and then started climbing a slight rise. The forest began to fundamentally change. The evergreen trees all but disappeared, replaced by sparser deciduous trees. Huge giants of trees. They still provided a canopy over them, but it was thinner and allowed some green-tinted light to shine through.

With the change in the forest, the trail ran straighter and they could see farther ahead. They could also smell something. The air became more and more humid and carried the smell of a rank, stagnant swamp.

"Remember that trip we made to the Great Dismal Swamp with the families a few years ago?" Paul said. "Something smells a lot like that."

"Not liking this," Amy said. "We really aren't equipped for a swamp. Maybe we should go back and try the other trail."

"Can't believe that's coming from you," Paul said. "Let's go a little further."

They continued, and the dank, fetid swamp smell became stronger. The trees changed from maple and oak to cypress, and they found themselves on the fringe of the black, still water of a swamp. The trail, though, continued on via small wooden bridges that spanned the gaps over the water and connected hillocks, small islands, and dry ground. Paul scanned ahead, trying to sort out where the bridges went. He thought he saw a small building out on a larger hillock, but couldn't make out details.

"Those bridges don't look too solid," Amy said.

"There's a shack out there, I think," Paul said. "Let's go just far enough to check that out. If it doesn't look promising, we can go try the other trail."

"Okay, but only one person at a time on those bridges," she said. She smiled. "You go first."

Paul approached the first bridge and tested it with his right foot. It seemed solid enough. He stepped out on it. Aside from a bit of jiggling, it held his weight and he made his way across. He stood on the hillock and looked back at Amy.

"I'm coming," she said. "But if I get wet, you're in trouble."

She walked across with no incident, but Paul noticed small ripples appear on the surface of the black water near the bridge. He'd seen ripples like that in lakes with large trout, but you could see the trout under the surface. The water here was inky black. He didn't want to fall in that water, and he didn't want to know what made those ripples either.

"Something is in the water here," he said. "Don't get close to it. And don't fall in."

He turned and crossed the hillock to the next bridge. He tested again. It was wiggly but sturdy, and he crossed it. Amy followed when Paul was successfully across. They repeated this process several times and finally came to a larger island with the small shack.

The shack was made of clapboard and built on stilts about four feet high to keep it dry in case the water rose. A set of rickety-looking steps led up to a door. There was a small window next to the door. Paul went up to the door and knocked.

"Anyone there?" he shouted.

There was no response.

He looked at Amy. She shrugged her shoulders.

Paul climbed the stairs. They were stronger than they looked. He tried the door. It opened and he peered in.

The shack was simply furnished. There was a table across from the door. To the right was a fireplace with a large chest next to it. On the left stood a set of shelves; a cot lay against the front wall under the window. The rough wood floor had no rug.

Paul entered. The shelves were bare, but there were a couple of plates on the table. The fireplace was empty and cold, with a stack of wood to the left. He looked at the chest. In contrast to the shack, the chest was pretty nice. It was made of brightly finished wood, with heavy leather strapping, brass fittings, and an ornate latch.

Paul used his staff to flip up the latch and then open the lid.

"You've played too many dungeon games. You expected a trap, didn't you?" Amy said.

He nodded. "Well, it is a pretty nice chest for this rickety little shack." He looked inside the chest. "You have got to be kidding me. Look, Amy!"

Inside there were two ornate flasks filled with a red elixir, two similar flasks filled with a blue elixir, a rope, a small pile of gold coins, two small leather pouches, and a scroll.

"Hmm," Amy said. "I feel like I'm about to level up."

Paul looked at her, then reached in and gently picked up the scroll. He took the ribbon off and unrolled part of it.

"This is a spell scroll," he said. "Can't make sense of it, though."

Amy looked over his shoulder.

"I can read it just fine," she said. "It's a scroll of fire dart. Basic magic user weapon spell."

"You can read this?"

"Yes."

"It just looks like gibberish to me."

"Well then, you're probably not a magic user. Your Intelligence and Wisdom scores aren't high enough. You probably have higher Strength, Dexterity and Endurance scores."

Amy held out her hand for the scroll, and Paul gave it to her. She unrolled it completely and read it.

"Yeah, I can do this," she said. As Paul watched, Amy glowed briefly. She then put the scroll in her pack.

"Are we now in a live game?"

"Yes, I think so," Amy said. "I should take the mana, or blue, potions. You take the healing potions and the rope. We'll split the gold."

She reached into the chest and started distributing the items.

Paul was a little mystified. Amy seemed to roll with this much better than he did.

"Should we continue through here?" Paul asked.

"I think so," she said. "Now I feel like we picked the right path. I'd hate to think what the other path had in store for us."

"Well, we can bull through this as far as we think we can go. If we're lucky, we'll come out nearer our goal."

"I want to see where this goes," Amy said. She held out a small pile of gold coins and a leather pouch. "Here's your share."

"Okay," Paul said. He put some in his pockets and some in a little leather pouch of coins in his pack. They shouldered their packs, picked up their staffs, and left the shack.

They continued crossing the small bridges, trying to see an end to the swamp in the filtered light. About an hour past the shack, while taking a food break, Paul heard rhythmic sounds in the distance.

"Listen," he whispered, looking at Amy. They could hear the sound of marching feet, some dim voices, and the rattling of equipment.

"Yeah, I hear it," Amy said. She got up and looked around. The hillock they were on wrapped around a huge cypress trunk on one side and had a thick clump of shrub in the middle. "This should work just like in the online dungeon games. The magic user is behind using the spells, while the fighter is in front taking on the ones who get through."

"You think this is going to be a battle?"

"You don't?" Amy said, smiling. "Make sure your health potion is in easy reach. I can't have you dying on me."

"What are you grinning about? And thank you for your concern. How many fire darts can you throw before you have to drink a mana potion?"

"I don't know. Right now I feel pretty charged up. I'm actually vibrating inside with power!"

"Hoo-boy!" Paul shook his head, then looked in the direction of the sounds. He could see vague figures moving. The voices didn't sound human and the language was rough and guttural. "This can't end well."

He set himself on what he thought would be a good place, near enough to the small bridge. He hoped to block the exit so he and Amy wouldn't get flanked and surrounded. Amy could work behind him, blasting fire darts at the opponents, and avoiding physical attack.

All he had was the staff. He was decent with it, but not as expert as Amy. Still, she had the fire darts and this was how the game was played in their online sessions.

The vague figures became less vague. About fifteen misshapen beings came across another bridge to the next hillock.

"Goblins," Amy said.

Paul saw the telltale greenish skin and ugly, knobby heads. The goblins crossed the bridge at a trot, then stopped on the other hillock. They weren't heavily armed and he was relieved to see no bows. He didn't see any armor other than a few helmets or a shield. Most carried short blades; some had clubs. Probably a raiding party or something. Still, there were fifteen.

"I think I'll start hitting them just as they cross the bridge," Amy said over his shoulder.

"Okay," Paul said.

One of the goblins pointed at Paul and Amy and started grunting and dancing around. He worked at inciting the rest, then turned and charged onto the bridge leading to Paul and Amy. He got about five steps onto the bridge when Amy's hands glowed blue and a huge dart of fire flew out and hit him dead center.

The first goblin went down on his behind on the bridge, smoke billowing from his leather shirt. He shook himself and got up. He was less steady, but started charging again. Amy hit once more. This time, he toppled lifeless into the swamp. After the body splashed, something in the water started thrashing. Some aquatic creature was enjoying a tasty snack of fresh goblin.

The rest of the group attacked. They could only cross one by one, and Amy took them out with yeoman's precision. It did take two shots, sometimes three before one went down. And by that time, the next one was even closer.

Paul decided moving a little further out on the bridge would be good. A goblin that had survived two darts was still coming. Paul spun the staff and knocked him in the head and into the swamp. The next goblin got the staff in the center of his chest and went backward against the goblin behind him. Both clattered off balance and went into the swamp.

From the corner of his eye, Paul saw one of those last two try to get to dry land, but was dragged back and under by something in the water. So, they had an ally in the swamp. Well, sort of. Paul didn't want to end up in the swamp himself.

Amy's fire dart finished the next goblin, and another dart flashed by to the one behind.

"Paul, I used one of the mana potions already."

He hadn't been keeping count. There were about eight more goblins attacking. One on one, he could hold his own with them, and his main goal would be to knock them into the swamp.

"Target the ones behind," he called out to Amy.

Paul went further out on the bridge and faced the attacking goblins. Two more met their fate in the water, and then the one with a shield was there. He also had a short blade.

The goblin deflected Paul's attacks and was able to counter with either the shield or the small blade. He delivered heavy blows with the wooden shield and cut Paul several times. Paul fought through, ignoring the pain of the cuts, and found a way through the shield defense. He came under the shield, hard into the crook of the arm holding it, and then rammed his shoulder into the goblin's face. Grunting, the goblin fell into the water and became another meal to whatever was feeding below.

Breathing heavily, Paul turned to look at the last goblin on the bridge. As Amy's fire dart hit the goblin, he collapsed and became a smoking, smoldering ruin. Paul kicked the body into the swamp.

Several items were scattered across the bridge. A large leather pouch lay nearby. Paul picked that up and gathered what else he could, then went back to the hillock and Amy.

"Paul, drink a health potion! Now!"

He took one out of his pack, pulled the stopper, and drank. It tasted sweet and refreshing. A rush went through his body, and the wounds of the battle healed. He still had rips and tears in his clothing and bloodstains down his left side.

"You were bleeding and probably would have died in a few minutes," Amy said. "What did you gather?"

They looked in the large pouch. There were small bags of gold, several jewels, a couple of health potions, and another mana potion. Paul tucked the health potions in his pack and gave Amy the mana potion. They split up the treasure.

"Let's see if there's anything else on the other side of the bridge," Amy said.

They passed by some of the weapons, but Paul picked up a very nice dagger and gave to Amy. He took one of the small goblin swords for himself. It was a short, broad blade, heavily rusted and covered with nicks, but serviceable enough and better than nothing. He strapped the sword onto his pack, putting the handle within easy reach. Amy arranged the dagger's sheath on her pack's shoulder strap, blade end up. She tested this arrangement. With a quick grab, she had the blade out and ready.

"You're getting downright deadly," Paul said.

"You're doing just fine, yourself," she said. "But this must be just the beginning."

"Yeah, we both know how it goes. If we continue here, things will get tougher and tougher. This may be the only way out, though."

"If we go back and the last trail is just a dead end," Amy said, "we'll just have wasted a lot of time, and maybe ruined our chances."

"Or we could be wrong."

"Don't lose faith now, Paul."

"I'm trying not to," he said, his head down.

Amy put her arm around his neck and held his head close to hers, then started a prayer. "God, we need Your guidance, Your grace, Your blessing." At the end, Paul said, "In Your glorious Son's name,

Jesus Christ. Amen."

He looked at Amy a moment, his hand on her face. He smiled.

"Thanks," he said.

"Thank you," she said. "You don't know how much I depend on you."

He stood straighter and looked around, then back at Amy.

"Let's go." He led the way across the hillock to the next bridge.

CHAPTER TWENTY-ONE
Village

AS THEY progressed through the swamp, the bridges became shorter and the hillocks larger, until they could see a much larger piece of dry land. The trail then climbed up into higher ground. It was more like walking in a normal forest. The trail wound through the hills and woods in a leisurely way. After a couple of hours, the hills gave way to more level ground and farms. Smoke drifted up into the sky from chimneys of the farm cottages.

The trail turned into a dirt lane with wheel ruts, and they overtook a man driving a pony and cart loaded with farm produce.

"Hello," Paul said as he caught up alongside the cart.

The man jumped in his seat and looked over at them. He stood and drew rein to stop the cart, then looked behind down the lane.

"Where did you come from?" he demanded, turning back to them.

"We crossed the swamp and the trail led up here," Amy said.

The man sat heavily on the cart seat, eyes wide. "You crossed the swamp?"

"Yes," Paul said. "It wasn't easy. There were some nasty goblins down there."

"Those goblins have been raiding and harassing us for years from the swamp. Nothing good has ever come from there. They steal our crops and drive off our stock. Why are you here?"

"I'm on a mission, and this just happened to be the way we came," Paul said. "But there are no more goblins left down there."

"No more goblins?"

"That's right," Amy said.

"Where did they go?"

"Oh, they're dead," Paul said. "They attacked us and we killed them. Most are making a meal for whatever creature is living in that swamp."

"There were more than just two or three goblins in that cohort," the man said. "You say that you two children defeated all of them?"

"Now you're getting it," Amy said.

"Where are you headed with all that produce?" Paul asked.

"Town. I sell it at the market in town."

"How far is it to the town?"

"About an hour down the road, my speed. Walking's faster."

"Thanks for the information," Paul said. He and Amy started walking again. When they got out of earshot from the man and his cart, Paul gave a quick glance back. "I think we rattled him a little."

"Well, he's a non-player character in this game," Amy said. "He's a simple farmer, so you can't expect much. Remember how limited and dull the NPC's in the online dungeons were?"

"Oh, yeah," Paul said.

They saw the village from a distance as they approached. It had simple log and wood buildings with thatch roofs, dirt streets, and brightly painted wooden signs hanging over doors of businesses. People bustled about on errands and tasks. The center of the village held the market, where farm produce, meats, furniture, and other kinds of products were sold and traded.

One of the buildings that didn't have a thatch roof was the smithy. A constant ring of hammer on anvil carried across the marketplace.

"Who do you think we need to contact here?" Paul asked. He looked at the village sign as they entered, but couldn't read the language. "Obviously, this isn't Choteau."

"No, I suppose not," Amy said. "Well, first, we should find a spiritual leader or a mayor. One of those people may have a clue how to get out of here. Otherwise, I think we find what passes for an inn. The common room is notoriously good for gossip and information. At least, that's always been the rule in the role-playing games."

"Good plan," Paul said. "Can we afford an inn?"

"Absolutely," Amy said, huge grin spreading across her face. "With hot baths!"

They made a circuit of the village and market, finding the primary buildings and making inquiries at a couple. They found the mayor, but he wasn't much help. A building that served as a chapel or temple housed the spiritual leader. This person, it turned out, had a little more information.

"Well, my children," the old priest said, "there is a portal to the north. We believe this leads back to your world. But it is a dangerous and difficult journey. It is not easy to find. I do have a good map."

"Oh, good!" Amy said. "Could we see it?"

"Yes," the priest said, "if you can meet the price."

"The price?" Paul said, suspicious.

"I need three hundred gold for the map. It is a precious item."

"Oh," Paul said.

"We have other business to do. But thank you," Amy said. "We'll discuss this and get back to you by tomorrow."

Amy rushed Paul out of the temple before anything else was said.

"That's a pretty steep price for just a map," Paul said as Amy led him at a fast walk down the street.

"We have the gold--or will--but I didn't want him to know that. We can probably get that map for a lot less with a bit of haggling. We have to sell a bunch of gems and jewelry. And I want to see if we can find another combat scroll or two. Fire dart will only take us so far. If things get tougher, we'll need better tools."

"How about weapons and armor?"

"Yes, we should find you some leather and a better sword. Don't get too excited, though. This is just a little village."

A local healer and herbalist lived in a hut close to the market. Inside were racks of flasks for healing, mana, and some other liquids Paul couldn't identify. He kept his hands in his pockets.

Amy spotted a shelf of scrolls and immediately started talking with the healer about what she might have. After a few minutes, she dug out her pouch of gold and exchanged a pile of coins for two scrolls and two more mana flasks.

Back outside, she said, "I found out who deals in gems and jewelry, too."

Across the market sat a larger hut with an ornate door. Inside they found a counter with lamps set along it to light the gems and jewelry that lay in small boxes lined with black cloth. There were amulets, too. Were any of the amulets imbued with power and in their price range? Paul doubted it.

He and Amy pulled out the gems and jewelry they had gathered and laid them on the counter as the proprietor approached.

"What do we have here?" he asked. "Oh, those are some nice baubles." He fingered through the items, picking up a large red ruby and holding it up to the light of a lamp. He set that one down and picked up a sapphire. He waggled it in the lamp light, and flashes from the star in the gem lit his eyes. About twenty minutes later, the proprietor had examined almost all the loose gems. He hadn't paid much attention to the rings or amulets.

Paul looked at the rings. One was a simple gold band set with a small emerald. Paul had always liked emeralds. He was appreciating the ring's simple craftsmanship when the proprietor coughed and held out his hand. Paul gave him the ring.

A few minutes later the proprietor gathered all the gems in one pile. Then he separated some of the other jewelry into two piles and held up the emerald ring.

"I will give you nine hundred and seventy-five gold for the lot," he said. "Nice gems, some costume jewelry. That ring, though, is imbued with something. I can tell that. I would offer you six hundred gold for it, but I think the young man should wear it."

"That sounds fair," Amy said. "The healer said you were honest and would pay honestly. And thank you for the advice about the ring."

Paul took the ring. A tingle ran through him as he slipped it on his left middle finger. *So,* Paul thought, *this is what it feels like to get a ring that improves some characteristic in a game. It kind of tickles.*

CHAPTER TWENTY-TWO

Tapestry

THE INN was built of stone and timbers, with the guest rooms above the common room, and a slate roof covering the whole thing. The innkeeper, a portly gentleman with a jolly smile, introduced himself as Robert.

He led them upstairs to a clean room with a small fireplace on the outside wall, two comfortable-looking beds, and a small table with two chairs. From a corner, he pulled out a large copper tub. "The house staff will bring the hot water before dinner for your baths."

"Thank you, Robert," Amy said, taking the room key from the innkeeper. "What's for dinner?"

"Oh, a fat juicy grouse, stuffed with rice and nuts, with potatoes and carrots on the side," he said. "And we have a cider that is only a very little bit hard. Perfect for your age."

"Sounds wonderful," Amy said. "We look forward to it."

Robert left, singing as he went. Neither Paul nor Amy had ever heard the song, but they appreciated his tenor.

"We'll visit the smithy before we go for the map tomorrow," Amy said. "We might be able to get you a decent sword."

Amy and Paul dug their pouches out and sat at the table to take stock of their fortune.

"Depending on the game system we're in," Paul said, "we could be very rich. How much was the room, meals, and bath?"

"Twenty gold," she said. "And it seems we're paying the premium rate."

"While you're bathing, I'll go down and see if I can learn

anything," he said. "I might even have a sip of that cider."

"Whatever you do, do not get cornered. And keep an eye on your drink at all times."

She pulled out the two scrolls she'd bought earlier. "One of these is a healing spell, and the other is a kind of missile defense; it protects us from arrows, darts, spears, and rocks. I figured we may need the healing for both of us, along with all the mana potions I can carry. Arrows and spears are things we haven't faced yet, and those things would end our mission quickly."

She opened and read each scroll. Her hands glowed as she rerolled them.

"I can do those. No problem. And I think I'm about to level up, which means all of the spells will be more effective, but cost more mana."

"This was so much fun when we all played online," Paul said. "Now it's life or death. Pretty real. Well, about as real as this twisted reality delivers."

He looked around the room.

"Robert said something earlier about a lockbox," Paul said. "Where is it?"

Amy got up and looked around, then went to the fireplace. She swung a fake stone out from the fireplace facing and found a metal door behind it. A small, second key on the loop with the room key opened it. They put their gold pouches inside and locked them in.

"And get your dirty clothing out. They'll take it to the laundry," Amy said.

"Good thing. I'm on my last set of nearly clean clothes."

A knock sounded on the door just as Paul finished piling his dirty clothes on his bed. He opened the door and saw some house staff with buckets of steaming water.

"Have a nice bath, Amy," Paul said as he left.

#

The common room had just a few people, all at one table, talking and sipping ale. Paul chose a table away from the group, but close enough to eavesdrop. He could still exit the room quickly if he needed to. A woman in a dark, full skirt and embroidered white peasant blouse came over and asked him if he wanted ale.

"I'd rather have some of the cider, please." Paul said. He had never tasted beer or ale and didn't want to start now.

She left with a smile and a swish of her skirts, and returned shortly with a leather mug brimming with a spicy apple cider.

Paul gave her a coin and took a sip of the brew. Just a hint of alcohol, but very good.

"Hey, laddie," the woman said, tossing the coin up and catching it again, "for this you can drink all night, and then some, and still have coin left over." She swished her skirts again as she turned and walked away. Paul felt the heat of a blush on his cheeks.

"That's what he said," a man was saying in the group nearby. "They came from the swamp and said all the goblins are dead." Paul didn't turn, but sipped quietly and kept listening.

"All dead?" another member of the group asked.

"Yes. No more attacks from the swamp--and that means more produce from the fields. We may be opening even more fields."

A movement caught Paul's eye on the wall to his left. A tapestry depicted the farming country with a lane running through it. In the middle of the tapestry a man drove a horse-drawn cart loaded with farm produce. He moved along the lane slowly. From the lower left corner of the tapestry came two figures who overtook the man and his cart, stopped a moment, and then continued on their way.

Paul stared in wonder at the tapestry, watching the changes as the men in the group talked. *That is so cool,* he thought.

"Who are these people you're talking about?" another member of the group asked.

"They were two children," the first man said.

"Children, eh?" said the other man, eyeing Paul.

"Doesn't seem possible. In any case, we are going to gather some men and go into the swamp to check this out tomorrow," the first man said.

Paul sat and sipped and listened to the group cover a number of other topics important to farmers and small village residents. As the topics changed, so changed the tapestry. As they talked about village issues he could see the layout of the village, and when they talked about the road north, the tapestry changed to the section of the village where the road led north.

Paul burned the image into his memory.

The group started to break up. One man stayed behind, though, and came over to Paul's table. He pointed to the tapestry.

"I see you found that interesting," he said.

"Fascinating," Paul said, then waved his hand to an empty chair. The man sat.

"I'm Joshua," he said, "a weaver. That tapestry has been hanging here for more than four generations. No one knows who made it or what enchantment causes it to show what it does."

"Nice to meet you, Joshua. I'm Paul. What that tapestry does makes it hard to have a private conversation in here, doesn't it?"

"Yes, but it keeps away those with evil intent. You see, anything they plot is exposed there."

Paul nodded.

"You're one of the children who came through the swamp, aren't you?" Over Joshua's shoulder, Paul could see the tapestry change to show the trail of bridges through the swamp. "You're not from around here."

"Yes and no. I came through the swamp with my friend. We're trying to get back where we belong, so, no we aren't from here. An old priest said he had a map to a portal, but he wants a lot of coin for it."

"Ah, old Angus," Joshua said, slapping the table and laughing. "Yes, he tries to sell that map to anyone who will pay. He has several copies. He makes them himself."

Paul laughed. "So he's using the map for his retirement plan." He glanced up at the tapestry and saw that it showed a route from the village to a location to the north. Paul tried to memorize the main landmarks of the route.

Joshua noticed Paul's attention to the tapestry and laughed. "You're a shrewd young man."

Paul thanked him and smiled. One of the house staff came into the common room and waved to Paul, then pointed upstairs.

"Sorry, I have to go. It was good meeting you, Joshua." They shook hands and Paul left.

#

Amy was finished with her bath and the staff had cleaned out the tub. They were already bringing up buckets of steaming hot water for Paul's bath. When there was a moment alone, Paul told Amy what he'd heard and seen in the common room.

"I know the basic route and landmarks," he said, "so we can use that for bargaining leverage, or just not worry about the map."

"I'd be more comfortable having the map," Amy said. "We can bargain."

"Check out that tapestry while you're down there," he said. "Pretty interesting."

Amy went downstairs and the staff brought in the rest of the water for Paul.

When they left him alone, he braced a chair against the door and undressed. The bath was almost too hot. He soaked for a bit, letting the heat relax and restore him.

#

When he was finished and dressed, he opened the door to signal the staff. Amy returned and they prepared to go to dinner. They left the room locked and entered a now bustling common room. They found a table and ordered their meal.

Paul looked up at the tapestry. With so many topics flowing in the room the tapestry just displayed waves of colors and patterns.

"When I first came down, I saw the tapestry was blank," Amy said. "I was alone. As soon as some other people came in, images started to appear. When more groups were in the room, the images on the tapestry got like this. I guess it's overwhelmed."

The meal arrived, and the innkeeper's description of the fat grouse was apt. Generous portions of potatoes and carrots also graced the plate. The waitress set down utensils and two mugs of cider and winked at Paul. He smiled in return.

Amy thanked the waitress and kicked Paul under the table. When the waitress was gone, she said, "This looks wonderful. I'm so hungry."

Paul discovered he was hungry, too. They ate in silence. Neither looked up until the grouse were reduced to bare skeletons on the plate with only small pieces of potato and carrot remaining.

"I'm probably going to sleep like a rock tonight," Paul said.

"Me, too," Amy said, rubbing her stomach. She sipped some of the cider. "This is really good."

"Just don't drink too much. It is a little hard."

They were pushing their plates away when someone approached their table. It was the man they'd met on the road that morning.

"You are the ones who cleared the goblins out of the swamp," he said.

Heads nearby turned, and more turned as the words were repeated in a whispered buzz across the common room.

"Hello," Paul said. "I see you made it to the village and the market. How's business?"

"Business is good," the man said.

People gathered to get a better look at Paul and Amy. Paul glanced at the tapestry. The image from the lane through the farms, with the man driving his horse and cart, was back.

"So how did you get through the swamp?" someone asked.

"We fought our way through," Amy said. The image on the tapestry shifted to the battle at the footbridge.

"But you're just children," someone else said. "How could you fight your way through all those goblins?"

"It wasn't easy," said Paul. "But we forced them to come at us one at a time. So it was actually two against one . . . uh . . . most of the time."

More questions came. The people were friendly and animated, and Paul and Amy enjoyed their celebrity status for a while. As the evening lengthened, the crowd slowly thinned. Finally, the last of the villagers left after handshakes and good wishes.

"I'm exhausted," Amy said. "Time to turn in."

They went up to the room and prepared for bed, taking turns down the hall. Paul braced a chair against the door again and opened the window to let in some fresh air.

Amy was already asleep and Paul fell asleep shortly after snuggling into his warm bed.

CHAPTER TWENTY-THREE
Brigands

A RAP at the door brought Paul awake. Sunlight streamed through the open window, and the chair had been moved aside from the door. The other bed was empty, so Amy was already up.

"Breakfast," came a voice outside the door.

"Just a moment," Paul said. He got up and pulled on his jeans.

Amy had locked the door when she went out. Paul opened it and the house staff brought trays in and set them on the table. They also brought in two bundles of freshly laundered clothing and set them on Amy's bed. Paul paid each of the staff one coin and thanked them all.

When they'd gone and the door was closed, he checked out the breakfast. Under the lid he found fruit, poached eggs, ham, and warm bread. There was also a pitcher of water with two cups.

He decided not to wait for Amy and dug in. He made quick work of his portion of the ham, eggs, and bread. He was biting into a fresh, ripe pear when Amy returned.

"These people do not have coffee, do not know what coffee is, and have nothing even close to it," she said. She went straight to the table and started on her breakfast.

"Where have you been?"

"I had to go to the bathroom," she said around a mouthful of ham. "Then I went down to see if there was some coffee. They have no coffee, did I tell you? And then I had a conversation with the tapestry."

"Oh, really?"

She filled a cup with water, drank some, then looked at the cup. "Not coffee," she said. "It turns out the tapestry does more than just reflect the current topic of conversation. It can actually respond to questions and statements directed at it, especially from someone like me."

"Someone like you?"

"A magic user."

"Oh, yeah."

She pulled a small paper out of her shirt pocket. "So I got the information we need and I made some notes. We don't need to buy the map, and I don't trust that priest."

"Good," Paul said. "I don't trust him either."

He finished his breakfast and gathered his toothbrush and other things. "My turn for the bathroom."

"Okay, but knock when you come back," Amy said. "I'm going to change into clean clothes."

She was ready when Paul returned. She gathered her toothbrush and things and went down the hall while Paul finished dressing. He was packing up his clothes and gear when she returned. They opened the lockbox and retrieved their money pouches. When Amy had her packing done, they shouldered the packs, grabbed the staffs, and headed out of the inn.

"First stop," Amy said, "the smithy."

The village smith had a few weapons and Paul found a nice short sword that fit his hand and was well balanced. The ring on his left hand tingled when he held the sword. He asked about the blade and the smith told him he'd only recently acquired it as part of a trade with a stranger. It turned out the trade had included a fitted leather jerkin that fit Paul perfectly. The thick but supple leather would provide some protection to his torso and was easy to move around in.

Paul figured out how to strap the sword's sheath on the pack so he could easily reach the hilt over his shoulder and quickly draw the blade.

The tally at the smithy was six hundred gold. They paid the smith and gave him the goblin sword too.

They continued out on the north road.

"How long will it take to get to the portal?" Paul asked.

"Two days, maybe three. There isn't a one-to-one relationship between this world and ours, according to the tapestry. And we can only hope that when we come out, we're somewhere near Choteau."

"Maybe this is what the coyote meant," Paul said. "This might be what he placed in our path that we can't overcome. It's almost like the inn back there with the dinner and breakfast are our final meals. We're rested and relaxed, well-fed, and fresh. We're starting out thinking we know what we're doing. The question is, do we know what we're doing?"

Doubt and uncertainty clouded Paul's mind. He looked at the trail ahead. *I don't know where I'm going and I don't know what I'll face,* he thought, *and I'm afraid.*

Without turning to Amy, he said, "I've been expecting, hoping to get a visit from Gabriel again. I just hope he knows where we are. I hope God knows where we are."

"I hope God knows where we are, too," Amy said. "We need his spirit and blessing to get through this."

"Something's been bothering me."

"What's that?"

"We've been fighting all these different opponents. Monks, samurai, aliens, goblins," Paul said. "We've been killing these people, these beings. I feel bad about it. I try to keep focused on the mission and I know God has his hand on my shoulder. But . . . "

"I feel bad, too," Amy said. "Believe me, blasting out that fire dart takes a lot more than just mana from me. On one hand, I know we don't have much of a choice. I mean, if this isn't self-defense, I don't know what is. But like you said, it's killing. Sometimes I wonder if we'll be forgiven for this."

"During the fight, I was more scared than concerned about what was happening to the goblins. I didn't even really feel it when I got stabbed or cut."

"Yeah, that's one of the reasons I got the healing spell. But there's something I need to tell you. The tapestry showed me more than just landmarks. There are worse things than goblins ahead."

"Oh, boy."

"I think we have the tools we need. You have a good sword, I have good combat spells. If we work together and keep close, we should be able to overcome whatever we meet."

"It does look like a good sword, but I don't know how to use it."

"We'll get a chance for you to practice a bit," Amy said. "You might keep the staff in your left hand and the sword in your right. You can use the staff as a kind of shield. You were getting pretty good using the staff, so it shouldn't be too difficult a change."

"Good idea. When I first picked up this sword, the ring tingled on my hand."

"Maybe the ring is an enhancement for you with a sword. The jeweler gave you good advice."

They walked through farm country, orchards, and vineyards. The fields were divided by stone or shrub fences. People working the fields looked up as Paul and Amy passed. Some waved, and they waved back.

Near midday, the farms, orchards, and vineyards thinned and disappeared behind them, giving way to rolling, open country with stands of forest or small woods and an occasional stone cairn at the top of a hill.

They paused for lunch alongside the trail where thick grass, stones, and some fallen trees made a natural picnic area next to a small stream. Paul practiced with the sword and staff. It seemed a good combination, and the tingling ring seemed to give him confidence and increase his skill.

Held in his left hand, and tucked under his arm, the staff made an interesting tool for parry and counterstroke, and didn't impact his ability to slash and stab with the sword. Still, he could drop the staff in a heartbeat if it became a problem or too complex to handle.

"What's the first landmark?" he asked, wiping sweat from his forehead.

Amy pulled her notes out of a shirt pocket. "A ruined watchtower on the top of a hill overlooking a river. The trail goes between the river and the tower. A band of brigands lives there. It's a perfect ambush site, good visibility from the tower for early warning. Traffic gets restricted to the narrow trail between the tower and the river. Natural barriers, like the forest, prevent going around. The tapestry said there may be as many as six brigands there."

"Forewarned is forearmed," Paul said.

"That's my thinking." Amy pulled out her three scrolls and read them, then rolled them up and replaced them in the pack. "I'm ready, though. I think we can take these guys. We have to."

"How far are they from here?"

"Not far, I think. Maybe less than an hour. We'll see the tower ruins before we get too close."

As they walked, Amy tested the missile defense shield. Paul noticed a crinkling of the air around them when she cast it, as well as a slight fuzziness at the edges of his vision. The spell lasted about ten minutes; then the effects went away.

"I can tell when it's about to expire," Amy said. "That gives me a chance to recast it before it fails."

"Good. We don't have any other defense against arrows. When it's in effect, I can still fight as normal, right?"

"Yes. Don't get too far in front of me and be careful of your peripheral vision. Make sure you look around when you can."

"Got it."

"It doesn't take too much mana, so I should be able to keep it in play without a problem."

When the ruins of the watchtower came into view, they paused in some trees on the side of the trail to plan their attack.

CHAPTER TWENTY-FOUR

Wolves

THE WATCHTOWER ruins provided a covered position from which archers could control the trail below. A blind draw to the right, on the back slope of the watchtower hill, probably hid the brigands' camp. From there, with a signal from the ruins, the brigands could send men to the tower or to either side to ambush travelers. The camp was probably well fortified, so attacking it directly would be difficult, if not foolhardy.

"We could come up on the back of the hill and take out archers in the tower ruins first," Paul said. "The shield will protect us from arrows until we can get at them. Then we draw out the rest, if they aren't already coming out of the camp."

"Good plan," Amy said. "I'll set the missile defense as soon as we're out of the trees here. We're probably in long distance arrow range by now."

They got quite a way up the back of the hill before anyone noticed they were there. The two archers on watch in the ruins started firing arrows at them. The arrows bounced harmlessly off the invisible shield.

As they neared the lower wall of the tower, a little red flag rose from the backside of the ruins. That must be the signal, Paul thought.

Amy cast fire darts at the archers, hitting them a few times, but they ducked behind the stones. The arrows were still bouncing off. Paul felt the crinkling of the air as Amy recast the spell. She was keeping back a little, making sure Paul was still covered by the shield, and giving herself room to cast fire darts. Paul headed to a break in the stones that would bring them face to face with the archers.

Inside the shelter of the lower wall, the two archers were still aiming arrows at Paul. As Paul came through the opening, they threw down their bows and took up short swords. Paul was ready and the fight was on. Amy launched fire darts as fast as she could. As many hit as missed in the melee.

Paul's staff blocked the sword attack of the archer on his left, and his own sword sliced across the chest of the other archer. He swung back with the staff and clipped the first archer's head. The archer went over in a heap. The second archer, bleeding freely, still tried to hack at Paul, but Paul lunged with the point of his sword and caught the man dead center. The sword slid in deeply, and the man was through.

The first archer groaned in pain, holding his head. Paul saw the telltale three-pronged fork on his wrist. He quickly checked the dead archer. He, too, had the tattoo.

"They're the Adversary's men," he told Amy. Paul dragged each man outside the back wall. He whacked the groaning archer across the head again and the man shut up.

The other brigands charged up the back of the hill. Paul counted five, one being another archer.

"Amy, keep the shield up," he called out. "I'm going to see if I have any archery skills."

He picked up one of the bows and a quiver. He found a good spot where he could fire over the back wall and started practicing on the advancing men. He got two down with arrows through their legs. A few more arrows netted one more wounded man, who broke off the arrow and continued to advance. Amy started firing the darts as the attackers closed, and Paul stood ready at the opening in the stones. The one attacking archer fired several arrows, but when he saw them bouncing harmlessly off the invisible shield, he dropped his bow and took up a short sword.

The opening in the stones of the back wall would force the attackers to come at Paul one at a time, unless they tried to climb the wall. Then Amy could burn them. She left one man a smoking ruin before he could reach the wall, and then she had to drink a mana potion. She fired a couple of more darts at the archer, and he stumbled to the ground.

One of the brigands came at Paul in the opening and fell to a shattering thump on the head and sword to the heart. Then the archer recovered from Amy's darts and stood, but found Paul in his face and Paul's sword in his chest.

Paul jerked the sword free and kicked the archer over. He moved down the hill to dispatch the two wounded men. They didn't ask for mercy; they growled and tried to attack him. Both died quickly. Paul cleaned his sword on one of them and put it away.

Amy came behind.

"Paul, you okay?"

"I'm okay."

"What happened to 'feeling pretty bad' about killing people?"

"Well, I keep seeing this tattoo on them," he said, nudging one of the dead men's arms to expose the tattoo on his wrist. "These are the Adversary's tools. Their whole purpose is to kill us. I'm not feeling so bad now. Besides, since the Adversary owns them, they're already dead in the spirit."

"You did okay with the bow and arrows," Amy said.

"Nah, I just got lucky."

"Let's go see what's in the camp."

They found two more health potions, two more mana potions, and some gold. Otherwise, there wasn't much else they were interested in taking with them. Most of the weapons and equipment had the three-pronged fork insignia, so they didn't even want to touch them.

They sorted out the plunder and got back on the trail.

#

"I think I leveled up when I smoked that one dude," Amy said. "After that, my fire darts were really hot!"

"I think I earned some points with sword skills and leveled up too. It seemed to just come naturally."

"What do you think all of this will mean after we get back to our world?"

"Probably about as much as it does when we play online. We have characters who gain riches, skills, and levels in the game world. Doesn't do a bit of good for us in the real world. I think the main thing here is to not get too wrapped up in it or let it influence our reality."

"You mean, as soon as we cross the portal to our world, we'll be just like we were?"

"Yeah, but still good-looking and smart." He grinned. She punched his shoulder.

"Well, as much as I've enjoyed being in the role of a magic user, I'll be glad to just be me again."

"Same here. I'll just be a fourteen-year-old kid with no combat skills. And that suits me just fine."

The trail roughly followed the course of the river. As afternoon became early evening, they looked for a good place to spend the night. Amy spotted a nice grassy place next to a stream. It backed up against a hill and was only open to the trail. One of them could keep watch easily while the other slept.

They settled in, and Paul gathered wood and used the Old Timer to whittle tinder. Amy set up a small campfire for warmth and light. They had a meager meal of what trail rations they had left, drank from the fresh, cold stream, and filled their bottles.

They rotated the watch through the night and slept well with no incidents.

"I wish for coffee," Amy said as she drowned the coals of the small fire in the morning. "Trail rations and water for breakfast. We got pretty spoiled in one night at the inn."

The sun was just above the horizon when they set out again.

"So what's the next landmark?" Paul asked.

"An abandoned village. The tapestry wasn't clear on what might be around there. If the distances are correct, we should be there about noon, maybe a little before."

"And after that?"

"After that comes the bridge. Two bridges, actually. The tapestry said the bridge on the map the priest tried to sell us is a trap."

"Whoa," Paul said. "I'm sure glad we didn't fork over the money for his map."

They paused on the side of the trail for a moment, and Amy got out her notes.

"The river and trail separate past the abandoned village. Then there's a fork in the trail. The bridge we don't want is to the right, and the one we do want is to the left. Going left puts the portal much closer, as well."

"So the bad bridge is a trap," Paul said. "But what do we know about the bridge we want?"

"Just that it's the correct bridge. I didn't get anything from the tapestry that indicated any bad monsters or brigands there."

As they approached the abandoned village, the forest surrounding them thickened, but it wasn't as deep and dark as when they'd first entered from the Montana countryside. It was mostly oak and maple, with some underbrush and the occasional evergreen. The terrain was still hilly, and the trail wound in huge arcs around hills and through woods.

Finally, they came over a rise and saw a large, bowl-like clearing with the abandoned village resting inside.

Most of the buildings were still standing, or mostly standing, but the thatch roofs were gone, leaving the support struts hanging over the empty spaces below. Grass and weeds grew over gardens, yards, and the market area in the center.

Paul scanned the village, looking for any sign of movement. The hair on the back of his neck stood on end and a shiver ran down his spine.

"I don't like this place," he said. "I wish the tapestry had said more about it."

"Yeah," Amy said. "I have warning bells ringing in my head right now, too. But I don't see anything down there."

Paul looked around the edges of the clearing. He couldn't see anything when looking directly, but things flashed in his peripheral vision. When he looked directly at a dark spot between trees across the bowl, he just saw the dark spot. When he moved his gaze to the side, he saw glowing red eyes.

He grabbed Amy's arm. "I'm seeing eyes like the coyote has, but I can't look directly at them. Look at that dark spot across the way. Then look away slowly."

"I see them," she said. "But you're the only one who can see the coyote. This must be some different evil thing."

"Wolves, maybe?" Paul scanned the woods surrounding the village. "There are more. I count eight." He wished he were a better archer. Wolves hunted in packs; they separated the weakest member from the prey group and killed it. Once he and Amy got separated, they would both be wolf lunch. In the real world, wolves rarely attacked humans, but this wasn't the real world.

"We can't skirt the village if the wolves are in the woods surrounding it," Amy said. "The only option is to go through the village and find a suitable building for defense for when they attack."

"Interesting how our options always boil down to a choice of one really bad thing," Paul said.

He looked over the buildings and saw one that looked promising near the central market. It had two doors and no windows, and it seemed pretty intact except for the missing thatch roof. The walls looked plenty high from his vantage.

"If we can get there," he said, pointing to the building, "and control the doors right away, we might succeed. I don't know if the wolves can scrabble their way up the walls enough to climb over, but it's worth a shot."

Amy pulled out her scrolls, gave them a quick once-over, and replaced them. "Just making sure things are fresh," she said. Then she made sure her mana potions were handy.

"I'll lead," Paul said. "I'm going to focus on the building so we don't get confused. You'll need to cover our backs in case any catch up right away. I counted eight out there, could be more I didn't see."

"Ready." She looked grim.

"Ready." He squeezed her hand.

CHAPTER TWENTY-FIVE
Bridge

PAUL SCANNED the woods surrounding the village one more time, then gave Amy a three-count. On three, they ran. Paul held his staff in both hands and Amy held her fire dart spell ready for a quick cast. They passed the first of the roofless, nearly collapsed buildings, and Paul caught a glimpse of gray and black flashing between houses on the edge of the village to his right.

The building they wanted lay just ahead. "We're going to make it," Paul said, but a large wolf walked across their path. Not pausing, Amy cast two quick fire darts at the wolf and Paul used the staff to break several of its ribs and knock it aside. They sped past with the wolf whining in pain and its fur smoldering from the darts.

Paul spun around in front of the building and let Amy pass inside. Several wolves loped up.

He jumped inside the building and shoved the door closed. Amy was already closing the other door. Paul looked around for something to brace that other door and found a post about six feet long resting upright in a corner.

"Amy, use that," he said, nodding toward it. He couldn't leave the front door; wolves were already banging against it outside. Amy got the post against the back door just before wolves bumped against it.

Some wolves scrabbled against the side of the building, trying to get over the top of the wall. It was just barely too tall, and Paul thanked God for that.

"How much of a space do you need to cast through?" Paul asked. "If I open the door just enough to cast fire darts at whatever wolf is there, would that work?"

"We can try." Amy positioned herself so she could cast through the partially open door when Paul opened it. He drew his sword.

"Okay," he said. "I'm only going to let them get a snout through. Ready?"

"Yes."

Paul let the door open about four inches, and a wolf tried to push through. Amy cast three darts and the wolf rolled away. Paul closed the door.

"Those were pretty powerful," Paul said. "How are you?"

"I'm good," she said. "I can do another before I need a potion."

They repeated the procedure, but Paul needed to stab once to finish the wolf. When the door was closed, Amy was on one knee and drinking a mana potion.

"Amy!" Paul said.

"I'm okay, Paul." She stood. "We can do this, but we just need to take our time. The wolves are magical or have a skill. When I cast against them, I lose something. A little mana, a little health."

"Do you need a health potion now?"

"No, I cast a healing on myself. I'm fine." She looked determined. "I'll be more careful between wolves."

"Okay, let me know when you're ready."

"Let's do this."

He opened the door again. This time, two wolves tried to push through. Amy cast darts and Paul stabbed with his sword until they fell away and he could close the door again.

"That was unexpected," he said, bracing against the door as several wolves banged up against it. Amy drank another potion, cast another healing, and shivered. The back door rattled as another wolf slammed against it.

"If we killed four here, and left one dying on the way," Amy said, "that's five. Sounds like we have at least four more out there."

"How many mana potions do you have left?"

"Four, I think. Enough."

"We might get two again, ready?"

She took a deep breath. "Yes."

He opened the door again and, as he'd predicted, two wolves slammed against it and tried to push through. They fought as before, with Paul hacking and slashing as best he could. When they fell away and Paul closed the door, Amy was on her knees and breathing hard. She drank a mana potion.

Paul pulled off his pack, dug out a health potion, and tossed it to her. She gratefully drank it down and shivered with the rejuvenation.

"They're draining me more each time," she said, finally able to stand. She drew some deep breaths and then nodded. "I'm ready."

They repeated the process, but only one wolf came to the door and he was dispatched quickly. Amy recharged with another mana potion and cast her healing spell. Things were quiet around the building. Then Paul heard a wolf snuffling around by the back door, then by the front. It padded around the building again. Paul moved from the door and let it fall open.

"Be ready," he said. Standing away, he held his sword and staff on guard. The last wolf came around again, stepping over the dead in front of the door. His growl came low and deep when he saw Paul and Amy. His eyes glowed red and he moved slowly into the room. Paul stood ready, his full attention on the wolf. It just continued to growl and watch the two. After a moment, it made a move to leave the room and Paul cut it off.

"No! You will not be allowed to go and then follow us."

The wolf leapt at Paul's throat, jaws wide. Paul shoved the staff into the wolf's mouth then stabbed up with his sword, piercing deep into its chest. The weight of the wolf knocked Paul back, but he was able to roll away. He stood and stabbed the wolf a few more times to finish it off.

He cleaned his sword on the wolf's fur.

Amy was on her knees again. Paul went to her.

"He was just standing there, sucking the life out of me," she said weakly. Paul grabbed another health potion and helped Amy drink it. She recovered somewhat. "I'll need one more."

He got it to her and she drank it down.

"There," she said. "Almost back to normal. I'll be better with some time, maybe some food."

Paul helped her up and they gathered their gear.

"Let's get out of this place," he said. "We can stop down the trail and eat something when we aren't weirded out by this village."

#

Sitting on a large rock on the side of the trail, they sipped water and munched some fruit Amy had gleaned from the inn. Paul wiped off as much of the wolf blood as he could from his clothing, but when they came to a stream he stopped, rinsed out his jeans, and changed into dry ones. His wet jeans hung off the back of his pack.

Amy was much better. The walk, and the food, seemed to fully restore her. She laughed when they talked, and smiled and shook her hair in the sunlight.

"Ah, this sunshine feels so good!" she said. "It's a pretty afternoon."

"Your spirits are well up now," Paul said. "Any more 'up' and we'll be flying."

She laughed again.

"Maybe I can bring you back down to earth, or whatever this place is. The next landmark is the bridge, right?"

"Yes. The bridge, but the correct bridge. We should find the fork in the trail soon. When we do, go left."

"Okay, so we get across this bridge, and then it's a straight run to the portal, right?"

"Assuming we don't run into something at the bridge. While the one on the priest's map is a trap, that doesn't mean the correct bridge doesn't have some challenge for us to face."

"We may have a challenge, but we don't know what it might be," he said. "Kinda like the abandoned village."

"Yeah, I just hope it's not more wolves." She shook herself and stood. "Time to move."

They came to the fork in the trail and went left. The trail wound through open meadows and woods and along creeks heading to the river.

Before long they caught sight of an arched, stone-and-wood bridge that spanned a deep ravine through which the river ran. They saw no building on either side, and the approach to the bridge was wide open.

Paul and Amy paused in some trees at the side of the trail and examined the approach. Nothing moved. Nothing seemed to be hiding in the nearby trees. Across the bridge it all looked the same.

"Maybe we'll get lucky?" Paul said.

"Maybe."

"All we can do is try crossing."

"The sooner we get across, the better I'm going to feel."

They started toward the bridge, keeping alert. Paul had his sword out. Nothing came at them from the nearby woods.

They reached the bridge and paused, looking around. All was quiet. Nothing moved.

Paul looked at Amy, then stepped on the bridge. Nothing happened. They crossed as quickly as they dared and soon reached the other side. The area around this side was clear, as well. Nothing moved or attacked them.

"God, thank You for this blessing," Paul said.

"Yes, to God be all the glory," Amy added. "Let's get to this portal."

"What do you know about the portal?" Paul asked. "Did the tapestry tell you anything about it?"

"Not much." She pulled her notes out. "The portal must be entered from the correct direction. Other than that, the map just has a compass rose that indicates north. There are no notes on the map about the portal. Just the symbol for it. The same symbol I drew in my notes from the tapestry."

She showed the notes to Paul. The symbol was a circle with a cross through the middle.

"Well, if the only indication on the map is the compass rose, we might guess that we need to go through while heading north," he said.

"Let's see what things look like when we get there," Amy said.

CHAPTER TWENTY-SIX
Portal

THE PORTAL site was also a crossroads, and Amy speculated that the trail to the right probably led back to the bridge that would have been a trap. The other two branches led off to the northwest and northeast. The portal itself was a flat, circular stone about ten feet in diameter, located just north of the crossroads on a slightly raised piece of ground. It was surrounded by stones convenient for sitting on, although that probably wasn't their original purpose. The air above the portal stone crackled with power and a blue haze floated there. Three concentric circles and a cross were carved through the middle of the portal stone. The cross was oriented to the primary compass coordinates.

"Okay," Paul said. "We'll only get one chance. We get in single file, walk straight across the stone's line to this reality's north, right down the groove of the line. If we both do the same thing, we should come out at the same place. At least, I hope we'll end up in the same place--in some reality, if not our own."

"You ready?" she asked.

"I guess. If we're wrong, at least we'll both be wrong and end up in the wrong place together."

A sound arose, of voices, growls, and people on the run. Paul stood and looked around. Down the trail to the right--the trap bridge trail-- came a number of brigands, heavily armed, followed by another pack of wolves, also on the run. Goblins were coming their direction from the other two trails.

"Well," he said, "our decision is made for us. We go or die. There are too many to fight."

He hustled Amy to the portal stone.

"You go first, Paul," Amy said.

"No. You go first, but I'll be right behind you. Go! Now!"

Arrows from the brigands' bows fell nearby. Amy went first, straight across the stone and along the groove. The color of the haze above the portal changed from blue to orange and back to blue, and Amy was gone.

Paul got on the stone and went across. An arrow clattered onto the stone next to him and a wolf growled just to his left. Then the world shifted.

#

Paul's legs continued to run, his arms pumped, and his pack bounced around on his back, but there was no ground. He was running through an expanse of gray, with blue veins of light running through it. He couldn't touch anything.

He seemed to be running for a long time.

"Please, God, let me come out at the same place as Amy," he said.

The gray lightened and became full daylight as he stumbled onto a road. A body slammed into him and arms wrapped around his neck.

It was Amy. He hugged her back.

"I'm fine," he said. "I'm here and we're fine."

She let him go and looked him over.

"Well, you almost weren't fine," she said, reaching around and pulling out two arrows that stuck out of his pack. "They almost got you!"

He looked at the arrows and raised his eyebrows. "Where are we?"

"I don't know," she said, tossing the arrows into the ditch. "But I think we're back in Montana. I can see a town up ahead."

A bridge to the northeast had a sign that read, "Teton River." They got off the road and Paul got the highway map out.

"Teton River," he said, "yeah, here it is. US 89 crosses it here. That's Choteau we see just up ahead." He looked around, then up at the sun. "And we still have most of the day left."

"Then let's walk."

Paul shoved his hand into his jeans pocket and pulled out a handful of what had once been gold coins in the other world. They were still coins, but quarters, dimes and nickels.

"Well, I could hope," he said. He reached up to where the sword was sheathed and pulled on the handle. The sword was unchanged, but the ring on his finger was made from a foil gum wrapper with a tightly folded green paper "gem" in the middle. It no longer tingled.

Amy pulled out what should have been flasks of mana potion, but just found some nice, ornate flasks wrapped in silver wire. Empty. Her dagger was flimsy plastic.

"Okay," she said, pulling off her pack, "I have to check."

She got out her scrolls, but they were just empty parchment. Their money pouches contained more quarters, dimes and nickels; the jewel pouches held some plain rocks. Amy tossed the rocks and the plastic dagger into the ditch.

"We have lots of loose change, anyway," Paul said. He checked his other pocket. The Old Timer was still there.

"You got to keep the sword," Amy said with a frown, then pointed at his chest. "And the jerkin. That's . . . good."

"Do I detect a note of envy? I like having this sword around. Maybe I'll keep carrying it after we get home."

"Yeah, pretty sure you'd get suspended from school for that. Expelled, even."

They crossed the bridge over the river and passed a farmhouse on the left. A man was outside working on a small tractor near the shop. When he saw them he came running up to the road.

"Hey! Where did you come from?"

"Just down the road," Paul said, pointing back the way they had come.

"Son, no one and nothing has come from that way, from the other side of the river, in three days! Anything that goes down the road that way disappears and we never see it again."

"This must be the real world side of the portal, then," Amy told Paul. "We came through the portal from the other side."

"Portal?" the man said.

"Several days ago, we entered something just this side of Vaughn," Paul said. "We just made our way through and came out here today."

"Where were you, then?"

"No idea," Amy said. "Some weird other reality."

Paul drew the sword and showed it to the man. "This sword

survived the transition to this world, uh, intact," he said, replacing the sword in its sheath.

"What did you need a sword for?" the man asked. "You're just kids."

"You wouldn't believe what we had to face there," Amy said.

"Where are you going now?"

"Choteau," Paul said. "I have something I'm supposed to do there."

"In Choteau?"

"Yes, in Choteau."

"Well, good luck," he said, turning to go back to his work. "I have work to do and a tractor to fix, portals or no. Not much in Choteau."

Paul and Amy walked on. They passed some houses on the right, then a large lumberyard on the left. Finally, they reached a sign that said "Entering Choteau."

They still had to walk a way before finding anything other than industrial or agricultural businesses. Once they were in the town proper and a few blocks down Main Street, they found a restaurant.

"I'm starving and we have some money," Paul said. "Let's get some real food."

"Sold!" Amy said.

They went in, found a table, and opened the menu.

"I'm getting the meatloaf with mashed potatoes and carrots," Paul said.

"I'm getting the grilled chicken dinner," Amy said. "And when we're done, we're ordering dessert. Not one dessert with two spoons, either. You get yours, I get mine. And I'm getting coffee."

The waitress came by and took their orders, which included two milkshakes that were on special. The milkshakes arrived in large heavy fountain glasses, with a generous amount of milkshake still in the stainless steel cups.

As they sipped on the shakes, a shadow fell on their table.

"I was wondering when you would get here," Gabriel said and sat at an empty chair.

"Where have you been?" Paul asked. "We could have used some advice and guidance recently."

"Again, I have to remind you, I am just the messenger." He looked the two kids over and glanced at their packs. Paul was almost embarrassed. His clothes had rips and tears. He and Amy were dirty.

"We know that, Gabriel," Amy said. "We just find your presence comforting."

"Thank you," Gabriel said. "It looks like your passage through the warp was intense. But you arrived here successfully. That is good."

"Well, yes," Paul said, "but we had to kill a lot of people and creatures to do so. How can this be part of the mission God placed on me?"

"Paul, you have had to navigate some dangerous and difficult things to get here. The Lord God's mission for you was to get to Choteau, where you have something to do to restore the world. Everything along the way has been the work of the Adversary."

"Even the aliens?"

Gabriel was silent for a moment.

"I think the aliens are an unintended coincidence. The Adversary's twisting of reality may have brought them here accidentally."

"Accidentally?" Paul said. "That is some accident. They're pretty destructive, but they aren't very bright."

The waitress brought their food and a tall glass of water for Gabriel.

"Paul, I know you struggle with the violence and killing," Gabriel said when the waitress left. "Know that what you've done is necessary. Those that belong to the Adversary are already lost. You should carry no guilt over that. That goes for you, as well, Amy."

He waved his hands over the food and said a blessing.

"Please, eat," he said. "We still have the last part of the mission to discuss."

#

After the meal, they left the restaurant and walked with Gabriel.

"This last part of the mission is here," Gabriel said. "Some miles away, there is an old, abandoned schoolhouse down Sherman Road. At this schoolhouse you will find a way into a tunnel. At the end of the tunnel is the reset switch. You must move this switch back to its normal position."

"Move a switch?" Paul asked. "That's it?"

"Yes, in a way. It isn't that simple, and the Adversary will oppose you."

"Why can't God move the switch?" Amy asked.

"It is part of the rules, as you might understand it," Gabriel said. "The rules as established between the Lord God and the Adversary. The Lord God gave you humans some precious gifts. One is free will. Another is His Son for your salvation, and the resulting Grace for those who accept that salvation. The Adversary, being who he is, has actually broken the rules in twisting reality."

Gabriel gazed upward. "The Lord God, being who He is, will not directly counter the Adversary, will not put His hand into this. So He placed this mission on you, Paul. You are free to complete this mission, or not. The Adversary gambles that you will choose to not complete the mission, that you will act in your own self-interest. The stakes are very high. The Lord God knows your heart. That is why He chose you."

They continued walking. Paul mulled over what Gabriel had said.

"What could be so difficult, now, that would make me give up the mission?" Paul said. "What could the Adversary do at this point to stop me?"

"Those are all questions for which I do not have answers. I can only tell you that you must be strong, stay faithful, and pray constantly to the Lord God."

Gabriel raised his hands and held Paul's head. He looked into Paul's eyes and Paul felt the flushing, cleansing power flow through his body again. After a moment, he let Paul go, turned to Amy, and repeated the blessing on her. Paul could see her glow with the power flowing through her. She went limp briefly, then Gabriel released her.

"This is as much as I can do to prepare and protect you," Gabriel said. "Know that you are loved, and that the Lord God has plans for you."

"Thank you, Gabriel," Paul and Amy said together.

Gabriel walked away and disappeared.

When Paul turned, he saw the street sign that read "Sherman Road."

"Ready?" Paul asked.

"As ever, I guess," Amy said.

They walked down Sherman Road.

CHAPTER TWENTY-SEVEN
Schoolhouse

THE ROAD left Choteau to the west and became a basic blacktop with few markings. Except when cars came by Paul and Amy just walked on the road. They passed houses and small farms and eventually reached the point where the blacktop ended and the road turned to dirt and gravel.

Gabriel had said the abandoned schoolhouse was "some miles" down the road. Evening was drawing near when Paul saw something not far from the road that looked like an old school--a simple, square structure with an empty bell cupola on the peak of the roof that leaned slightly. A large oak stood to the left, old and damaged from lightning. To the right, a copse of woods stood at the outer edge of what had once been the play yard.

"I think this is it," Paul said.

He and Amy turned off the road and approached the old schoolhouse.

Three figures moved from the left side, and three more moved from the right.

"Monks," Amy said.

"We know how to deal with them," Paul said. He pulled the sword out and took his stance with both staff and sword. "I just wish you could blast them with fire darts."

"Yeah," she said. She had her staff spinning and attacked the three on the right. Paul went at the three on the left. It was short and violent, but all the monks went down and then disappeared in puffs of acrid smoke. Paul and Amy turned and looked around.

"See any others?" Paul asked.

"No," she said. "But I'm not sure where these came from. They just sort of materialized."

Paul kicked the robes off to the side.

"They weren't any tougher this time, though," he said.

They looked around the schoolhouse. Windows and doors hung open or were gone altogether, but the main walls and framing were still intact. The stone foundation set the main part of the building up off the ground about three feet. Paul checked the steps up to the front door and they seemed still sturdy. The stairs to the entrance in the back were long gone and only small patches of whitewash provided evidence of the original color of the outside boards. Paul found no entrance through the foundation stones, so he figured a trap door or something must be on the main floor. They came back around to the front and looked at the main steps.

"These look solid enough," Paul said. As he approached the steps, something gray and tan moved on the edge of his vision.

He turned toward the copse of trees. "The coyote is here."

"What's it doing?" Amy asked.

Paul held the coyote's stare. "Just looking at us right now."

Amy moved close to Paul's side and kept a watch on their surroundings.

The coyote's voice slithered its way through Paul's head, leaving an oily trail across his mind. "So you think you are about to win, do you? That would almost be cute if it weren't so pathetic. You cannot complete the mission. It is too difficult for you and you cannot make the hard choices required. You are too young. You shouldn't have to make the hard choices. You are weak, tired, and dirty. You should just rest. Take a break. Think about things."

"No!" Paul said. "You're wrong. We will complete the mission."

"Ah, but there is no more 'we.' Only you can go. You have to leave precious Amy behind. She cannot follow you. When you leave her behind, my monks will take her. Amy will be mine--and not just Amy, but your parents and you little brother and sister as well. The instant you set foot in that schoolhouse, my monks will take them all."

Paul shook with frustration. *He can't take my parents, Roger, or Sarah,* he thought. *He can't take Amy. Can he?* There weren't any monks around that he could see, just the coyote with its red eyes glowing in the fading light. But the last batch of monks had come out of nowhere.

Doubts and the oily, slimy film left behind by the coyote's words clouded his vision. He was tired--exhausted, actually. Maybe he should rest. Take a break. What difference could a couple of days make at this point?

He took a deep breath. He couldn't abandon the mission or delay it. He had to complete it, because he'd accepted it. And he belonged to God.

Then he felt Amy's hand on his shoulder. "Paul, your sword," she whispered. "It's glowing!"

He reached up behind his shoulder and pulled out the sword. A bright glow flooded from the sword, bathing the schoolyard in blue light. The coyote twitched when Paul held the sword up. Amy's touch, warm, gentle on his shoulder, calmed him. *This mission,* he thought, *is more than just me, Amy, our families.* He thought of Jennifer, the minister in Billings. She'd said more than he knew depended on his completion of the mission.

It depended on him, Paul Shannon, because God had asked him to do it. He stood straighter and looked at the coyote.

"Deceiver," Paul said. "Every word that drips from your lips is a lie. You never give the straight story, you always twist it. Even when you attempted to deceive Jesus Christ he told you 'get behind me, Satan.' He knew you before and knows your work."

The coyote flinched at the name of Christ, with a slight yelp.

"Oh, but you don't know what you are up against, Paul," the coyote said. "I am equal to your God and when I win this conflict, I will take my place in the universe."

"You are not equal to the Lord God," Paul said, his arm raised, pointing the sword at the coyote. He felt the spirit move in him and he let it lead his words. "You may be immortal, but you are created by God. You cannot be His equal. You can only lie and deceive. You can only try to tempt us away from God and separate us from the Holy Spirit. In the name of the Lord Jesus Christ, I rebuke you!"

The blue glow from the sword brightened and the coyote took a step back. The red glow in his eyes flickered.

Then he drew himself up taller than ever. "Foolish boy! Did you not hear me? You have to leave Amy behind to complete the mission.

And when you do, I will take her, just as I took Joe. She will be mine! But if you abandon this mission, I can make you a ruler on this earth. You and your family, and Amy, will be safe and secure for all time. You will never know hardship again. You will live in comfort and peace."

Paul braced himself and raised the sword higher. *I could rule here? With Amy and my family?* He felt a pull to this idea. *I could rule, I would make the world a better place. I would bring peace and prosperity everywhere . . . Wait, what am I thinking?*

"All you offer," Paul said through clenched teeth, "are empty promises of comfort, riches, and worldly pleasures. You can't deliver real security, and you can't take that which is reserved for the Lord God. You lie. Amy is strong in her faith and is a loved child of The Lord God. She will fight you and will not yield to you or your lies. In the name of the Lord Jesus Christ, I rebuke you!"

At each mention of God and Jesus, the coyote flinched and whined, and when the second rebuke came, blue flames shot from the sword and he crumpled. Pieces of singed fur flew.

And yet again the coyote got back on his feet. He struggled at first, but then he seemed to regain his strength and grow even bigger and more menacing.

The voice in Paul's head grew to a roar. "I will send my minions against Amy. If she does not yield to me, she will die!"

"I may die completing this mission. Amy may die. But we will both find ourselves in the loving arms of Jesus," Paul shouted. This time the sword glowed brightly and the letters of the word "TRUTH" appeared along the blade in flames. "Your minions cannot defeat someone protected by the love of the Lord God. Amy lives in the Grace of Jesus Christ and has nothing to fear from you. In the name of the Lord Jesus Christ, I rebuke you!"

The sword flashed brightly and the coyote fell, with smoldering flames licking up from the ground at what was left of his fur. His tail was all but consumed.

Unbelievably, the coyote again regained his footing. He was outlined in flame now, a being of fire and fury.

"But she will die!" he said again. This time, Paul could hear a trace of a whimper in his voice. The eyes glowed fitfully now, and the legs shook.

"Liar!" Paul said. The words flowed from him. "You cannot kill her, you cannot take her, you cannot deceive either of us. We are children of the Lord God. We are protected by his love. You cannot touch either of us without permission from God. You will lose this battle. You deceive even yourself. You know that the Lord Jesus Christ's sacrifice for us, our redemption, means you have already lost your contest with the Lord God. You have already lost. And as a created being, you are subject to the Lord God, no matter how much you are given to pride and avarice. So in the name of the Lord Jesus Christ, begone!"

A roaring gout of bright blue flame launched from the sword and hit the coyote full-on. A mournful wail pierced the air and the coyote disintegrated in a pile of ash. The sword returned to its normal state and the dark afterimage of the schoolyard seemed dull and plain.

"I only got one side of that conversation," Amy said. "But it sounded pretty intense. What was the deal with all the yelling and the flaming sword?"

"I'm not sure. I felt something come over me. I think it was the Holy Spirit. It helped me say what needed to be said to the Adversary. We can rebuke him in the name of Jesus Christ. And in the name of Jesus Christ, we can tell him to begone!"

He turned and looked her full in the face. "Amy, you need to keep the faith and be strong."

"What are you talking about?"

"The coyote said I have to go alone," Paul said. "If that's true, I'll get my part of this done as quickly as I can, but you have to stand firm here until I come back."

"I can stand firm, I can fight, I can rebuke, I can even shout begone," Amy said. "What could happen when you go down there?"

"The Adversary will try to turn you, or . . . or kill you, while I'm down there. I don't know what he'll send or try to do. But if I have to go alone, I have to choose to complete the mission, Amy. I hope you know that."

"I belong to God," Amy said. "The Adversary can't do anything that will separate me from Him. I think that's the least of your worries."

"Let's see if we can find this entrance," Paul said.

He carefully climbed the stairs. Amy followed. They looked

around the floor of the one-room schoolhouse. The remains of old desks and other debris covered the floor. Paul kicked trash away as he slowly walked across the floor. Amy did the same, going around the outer edges of the room.

Paul found a board and used it like a shovel to move large amounts of debris. He was pushing a pile of dirt and chunks of wood when something stopped the board and it jammed into his hand.

"Ouch!" he said.

"What did you find?"

"I don't know." He got down on his knees and brushed debris away. "Hey, there's a ring on a large bolt over here!"

They joined forces to clear the area around the ring, eventually revealing a trapdoor in the center of the floor. Paul pulled on the ring to open the door but couldn't get it to come up more than an inch.

"Man, that's heavy," he said. "We need some leverage."

"Use your staff," Amy suggested. "See if that helps."

Paul put his staff about a third of the way through the ring and pulled up. He got the door raised a few inches.

"That worked," he said. "When I lift it, wedge some boards underneath to hold it. We'll work this little by little."

He lifted, and Amy pushed some wood under the corners. Paul lifted again, and Amy moved the wood and added more. After a lot of work, they got the door open about six inches.

"This is taking too long," Amy said. "We need something that will help us lift this."

Paul pulled off his pack, dug into it, and pulled out the rope they'd found in the little shack on the other side of the portal. Unlike the gemstones and gold coins, the rope was still intact and in its original form.

He looked up at the rafters. They looked sturdy. He tied one end of the rope through the ring, then tossed the rope over a rafter.

"Okay, Amy," he said, "you help lift with the staff while I pull on the rope. We should get some additional advantage here."

They pulled and lifted and got the trapdoor open another foot. The rafter creaked. One more coordinated pull and lift and they had another foot. The rafter groaned ominously. The door was now too high for Amy to get any lift leverage. She pulled the staff out and pushed from underneath, and they had the door up to five feet. She braced the door with her staff and Paul's staff on each corner. Paul loosened the rope and took the weight off the rafter.

Paul came around, breathing heavily.

"That is some heavy door," he said.

"Well, it's open enough to get through," Amy said.

"I guess that'll have to do." He thought a minute, then said, "No, this can't work, Amy. We can't leave both our staffs wedged in the door. What will you use to defend yourself?"

Paul looked at the angle of the door.

"Let's just push it over," he said. "It's almost upright now. You grab your staff and I'll grab mine and we'll push. We can do this."

They took hold of their staffs and pushed. At this point it took all the power they could manage just to move the door an inch, but they kept at it until finally the door moved to completely vertical. Then, with another push, the door fell back with a huge crash. The floor shook and debris and dust flew around the room.

The evening light was fading.

"The coyote said you won't be able to come with me," Paul said. "I don't see how that could be. Maybe it's a lie. It's getting dark, and I'd hate for you to be left here alone. Come with me if you can."

"Don't worry about me. I have some of Sal's matches left, remember? And I have my staff."

Paul took a deep breath. This was the final part of the mission.

"All I can do now is get the job done," he said. "Amy, if you can't come, be careful. I'll be back as soon as I can."

"Go, Paul," she said. "I have faith in you."

He stepped to the edge of the opening. Wooden stairs led down into shadow. He stepped on the first stair, then the second.

When his head drew level with the floor, he looked behind him at Amy. "The stairs feel solid. Grab your staff and follow me."

Before he'd even finished speaking, Amy, the trapdoor, and the schoolhouse had all vanished into an expanse of darkness.

CHAPTER TWENTY-EIGHT

Separated!

"AMY!" Paul shouted. "Amy!"

There was no reply. Paul reached up into the darkness above his head and met what felt like solid stone. There was no way back to the schoolhouse. The stairs kept marching straight up into the ceiling and then just stopped.

There was nowhere left to go but down.

Paul climbed down the stairs into a graying darkness. Finally, after about twenty or thirty steps down, he found solid ground. Something above and behind him glowed softly. He reached up and got the sword. It glowed just enough to illuminate where he stood and show the tunnel ahead.

Holding the sword in front, Paul moved down the tunnel. It went straight for a time, then curved one way, then another. At one point, the tunnel had a slight uphill incline. Then, after what seemed like an hour or so, the sides and floor of the tunnel became slick and damp with moisture. Small drips fell from the ceiling.

What's happening to Amy? Over and over the question played through Paul's mind. The coyote had said the monks would come after her. Was she fighting them now, alone, as he trudged underground, unable to help?

More stairs appeared, cut into the stone this time. By the sword's light Paul could sometimes see clusters of moss. It was cold. Paul climbed down, reached a landing, turned, and climbed down some more, again and again. His legs burned from the effort and he slipped and stumbled sometimes.

Just when he thought he could climb no more, the stairs ended and the passage leveled out. A light glowed ahead.

He approached cautiously, not wanting to fall into a trap. The light came from a small room at the end of the tunnel. A large, horizontal stone switch dominated the far wall. Paul stood alone at the only entrance to the room, looking at the switch.

He entered the room cautiously. So far nothing had attacked him since he'd gone through the trapdoor, and that made him suspicious. Even though his legs ached and trembled with fatigue, he knew this had been too easy.

The sword dimmed, but Paul kept it out and ready. Slowly he advanced into the room. Nothing leapt out at him. No monks materialized out of nowhere. No coyote appeared to tempt him to give up.

He moved closer to study the switch. It was set in a big stone rectangle like a giant switch plate. For all the stone facing, the whole thing looked pretty much like a light switch fixture in his home, just laid on its side. A stone bar, the toggle switch, sat in a notch on the right.

From what Paul could see, the bar would have to be lifted out of the notch on the right and moved across the slot, then dropped into the notch on the left.

For a moment Paul just stared, amazed that it could be this simple. Then he slipped the sword back in its sheath and tested the weight of the stone bar.

Nope, he thought, *it isn't that simple.* The bar was heavy. He dropped his pack, then got his back and shoulder under the bar and lifted with his body. Nothing.

He grabbed the bar to pull himself back up and noticed a deep, narrow slot in the end of the bar.

Paul inspected the entire room for anything that would fit the cut in the bar. As he came back by his pack, his saw the sword in the sheath. *Can't hurt to try,* he thought.

He drew the sword, took it to the stone bar, and slid the blade into the cut up to the hilt. Immediately a cool blue light shone out from the switch housing and from the sword.

He didn't want to break the sword, so he gently pushed up on the sword handle to test the weight. The bar lifted. It was still heavy, but it moved. He pushed it to the left and met considerable resistance. He leaned his full weight and all his strength against the bar and the sword hilt. Stone ground on stone as he pushed, and squealing broke the air as if metal were twisting.

Sweat beaded on his forehead and dripped down his nose, but still he pushed.

Then, to his left, a sliver of light opened up and widened, as if the movement of the switch were opening a door in the stone. Paul was so started he almost let go, but he kept pushing, and the sliver widened into a view of the schoolhouse.

Amy stood in the schoolyard, near a fire made of wood scraps from the schoolhouse and monk cloaks. She pushed some more cloaks onto the fire with her staff and turned. She looked tired. The dangerous look when she faced a fight was gone. Tears streaked her face.

Then twelve monks materialized in the schoolyard. Wearily, Amy lifted her staff and prepared to meet them.

It was more than an image. It was vivid, three-dimensional, real. Paul knew, without knowing how he knew, that he could step through the opening and be with Amy in an instant.

"Amy!" he yelled.

He hadn't meant to call out to her, not with twelve monks attacking. He'd done it without thinking. Amy looked up, her eyes wide with fear. He could see the monks reaching for her, the hoods falling back to expose sallow faces, slack jaws, and rotting teeth.

"Paul!"

The bar sat just inches from the left notch. Amy was facing twelve monks. Paul wanted to jump through the doorway to help her. He reached for the sword.

As his hand gripped the hilt, he paused. He needed to finish the task. How much of what he saw was illusion? Was it real? He was so close. Amy was in mortal danger and he could see his staff nearby. He could help her, but what would it cost? He could finish the task, but would he have time to help save Amy?

The switch had only about an inch to go, after all. *Please, God, give me strength,* he prayed. He put his shoulder and back into it and shoved. There was a lot of grinding and squealing. He could see the monks closing on Amy. Paul was exhausted, but he gathered his strength and pushed one more time.

The bar fell into the notch.

The blue light faded around the switch, and the doorway to the schoolyard disappeared. Paul pulled the sword from the bar and backed away toward his pack. More grinding, squealing, and clanking went on behind the switch. The switch morphed into the wall, which became one large blank solid stone. No evidence remained that the switch had ever existed in the first place.

I have to get back to Amy, he thought as he shouldered his pack.

He turned and left the room the way he had come. The way was still treacherous, and he slipped and fell several times going up and down stairs and along muddy tunnels. Would the trap door be there? Would he even find the stairs to the schoolhouse at the end of these passages? The sword provided feeble light to help him, but nothing looked familiar.

He stumbled and fell on the muddy tunnel floor, skidding along on his stomach and trying not to cut himself with the sword. His legs and arms shook with exhaustion as he struggled to get back on his feet. Then he bumped something.

Wooden steps. He prayed these were the last ones and that the trapdoor was just above him. He climbed the stairs in the darkness, the sword no longer providing light. Then the flickering light of a fire revealed the floor of the schoolhouse. He was climbing out of the trapdoor.

The fire in schoolyard silhouetted Amy sitting in the doorframe. Sleeping? He walked to the door and sat next to her.

She looked up from her half-sleep and smiled.

"Hi there, hero!" she said, throwing her arms around his neck and hugging him. "You succeeded!"

"Thank you," he said, hugging her back. "I feel wrung out."

"My goodness, you're dirty!"

"I thought I saw you through some kind of portal," he said.

"Yeah, I heard you call my name. There were twelve monks coming for me."

"I saw them. I almost jumped through the portal to help."

"Good thing you didn't. You finished the task. I knew you did because just before the monks were close enough to touch me, they evaporated. That's how I knew you succeeded."

"So it's over." Paul sat and put his arm around Amy. "I'm glad. I had to beg God for the strength to finish."

"We still have one challenge," Amy said.

"Oh?"

"How are we going to get home?"

"Well," Paul said, "If our parents are home in the next day or so, we can call and see if they'll get us plane or train tickets."

"And what excuse are you going to use for being in Choteau, Montana?"

"I have to think about that."

"After all this, it can't be that hard." She laughed.

CHAPTER TWENTY-NINE
Forward

THEY SAT next to each other, Amy with her head on Paul's shoulder, watching the fire, both exhausted. A glow started on the eastern horizon. Paul couldn't believe it was morning already. He got up and put more wood on the fire. He felt the predawn chill.

As he came back up from feeding the fire, he noticed that the trapdoor was closed. Then he looked again.

The trapdoor wasn't just closed--it was gone. His rope lay where the door should have been. There was no ring. There was just a space on the floor cleared of debris, with his rope coiled in the middle.

He told Amy about it when he came back. "That's interesting. It won't matter what we say to anyone, we have no way to show what we did. "

"We have to live by faith, Paul," Amy said. "You completed the mission by faith. That's all you need. When you tell the story, just tell it and let it do its work."

Dawn was coming, and they let the fire burn down.

"Any thoughts yet on how we get home?" Amy asked, yawning.

"No. But I think we should get our gear together and start walking. Just like we started this whole trip." Paul stood and brushed the dust from his jeans.

"Head back to Choteau?"

"Yeah. We still have some money and I bet that restaurant has some great breakfast. You never know, we might get a ride."

"It would be a start," Amy said, getting up and brushing off the seat of her jeans.

They gathered their packs and staffs and left the schoolhouse.

Gabriel walked up to them from the road.

"I don't think I'll ever get used to the way you just show up," Paul said. "But I'm always glad you do."

"Thank you, Paul. I'm just here to complete my part."

"What part is that?" Amy asked. "Got an airline ticket, train ticket, bus ticket?"

"No, I'm sorry, I don't have any of those. I do have a message. The Lord God is well pleased and wants you to know that you are his precious children."

"Thank you," Paul said.

"Yes, thank you, Gabriel," Amy said. "I feel right, good, kind, whatever, whenever you're around. That's pretty cool."

"Angels are around all the time," he said. "We do the Lord God's work. You can only see us when necessary."

"I wish you could be around more," Paul said.

"We have one more task to complete," Gabriel said, reaching out his hands to Paul and Amy. "Take hold of my hands."

They did as he asked and then seemed to be walking in a swirling cloud with a light breeze blowing their hair about.

"Your parents will be home shortly from Charlotte. You have time to clean up and be ready for them. As you already figured out, Paul, evidence of what you did is gone. What happened to the world is very real and there is great loss everywhere. The damage and loss of life are permanent. And, for you, Joe is gone. His parents will be traumatized, and you two will be a great comfort to them. An urn with his ashes will arrive at their home soon."

Gabriel gave their hands a gentle squeeze, then released them. They were standing at the small footbridge near their homes in North Carolina.

"We're home!" Amy said. "Thank you!"

"Thank you, Gabriel!" Paul said. "Thank you!"

"Thank the Lord God," Gabriel said. "Through Him, all things are possible. Always be thankful, children. I must go now."

Gabriel turned, walked away, then faded from sight.

"We're home!" Amy said to Paul.

"I hoped, but couldn't be sure Gabriel would bring us home," Paul said. "I almost couldn't face making the trip back. This is great."

Paul grasped Amy's hands and bent his head. He gave a prayer of thanks to God. Amy added her own thanks.

"We need to get home," Paul said, finally.

"I'll see you later, though," Amy said. "I'm sure our parents will want to get together to support Joe's parents." Amy gave Paul a quick kiss on the cheek and ran toward her house.

#

Paul opened the front door of the house. It was just as they had left it. He went up to his room and dumped out his pack on his bed. He put his dirty clothing in the hamper and hung the sword in his closet. He did not know why he still had the sword, but he was glad for that. It may never again glow and burn, but it would always remind him of what God might ask him to do.

He got the Old Timer out of his pocket and set it on his desk, near the lamp. Then he leaned his staff up against the wall near the door. The staff was scarred along its length and the ends were rounded from grinding on the roads and trails. But it was a comfort and he knew it would be something he would keep with him. He took off the leather vest and hung it among his other clothing.

He undressed and got in the shower.

#

Paul was sipping on a glass of water in the kitchen while listening to the news when his parents' car pulled into the driveway. He ran to the front door and opened it. Sarah and little Roger came charging out of the car with arms spread to hug him. Mom and Dad came up and hugged him too. It felt good to have his whole family back again.

They gathered around the kitchen table and shared their stories. Dad said that the last week was being called "The Troubles." Things had gotten a little intense in Charlotte. No one could get in or out and food started to get scarce.

"Still, we held together with Amy and Joe's parents and our other family and persevered," Dad said. "We heard about Joe, though, when the dome disappeared. This is going to be tough for his parents. Still, we are blessed. So many have lost so much during this time."

"Joe is in the arms of Jesus, now," Paul said. He told of their travel, what they'd run into, the people they'd met. His family asked a lot of questions, and Paul did his best to answer all of them.

"But the switch, the trap door, some other things," Paul said, "they're just gone. No way to show what happened."

Dad put a hand on Paul's shoulder. "You know what happened, and so does Amy, and so do we. That's all that matters. Now come outside and help me with the luggage."

"Sure," Paul said, smiling. Life was back to normal--or as normal as it would ever be now. He'd learned from the news that the national government was now a handful of people huddled in a special facility near Denver. Some of the major cities affected had been completely decimated. Fully two thirds of the world's population was gone, and small wars had broken out in many places as people became desperate for food, water, power, and other resources.

#

Later that day, the three families gathered at the home of Joe's parents. The Shannons and Grossmans brought food and love and comfort. Paul and Amy told how Joe had fought the aliens and how he'd been carried to Jesus by the angel Gabriel. Paul confirmed Joe's faith in God and his commitment to Jesus Christ and repeated that he knew Joe was in the arms of Jesus.

While they were gathered, the television was on in the living room. Paul saw that Washington, D.C., now free of the black fog, was all but empty, as was Rapid City. The white fog that had settled on Moscow and some other cities had left them completely empty as well.

The aliens had pulled out and seemed to have left with no trace other than a trail of destruction. Paul thought that made sense. If they were an accident, an unintended coincidence, as Gabriel had said, they may have been thrown back into some other timeline or elsewhere in the universe.

Cities that had stopped were back, but just shells with few survivors. Cities that had disappeared never came back. The monks had disappeared from Des Moines, Iowa, and the zombies were gone from Asheville, North Carolina, but the populations of those places were decimated. Reporters said that it was fortunate the zombies never got to other cities. It could have been an even worse apocalypse.

London was back to being dreary but much less populated; Paris had been emptied of frogs and most of its citizens; Mexico City no longer had snow, but the piles of dead were a huge health problem. Public utilities limped along in some areas, but distribution networks of supplies like food and fuel were nonexistent. What was left of local and regional governments, according to the reports, was mobilizing to restore everything, but estimates were that it would take years to recover.

"Remember what Joe said about the black fog?" Paul asked when he and Amy found themselves alone in Joe's back yard. "I thought it had killed him when it touched him."

"Me, too," Amy said. "He said he thought he knew what Hell was like."

"I miss Joe," Paul said.

"I do, too," Amy said, and wiped a tear.

Paul scuffed his shoe in the grass. "It's hard to imagine how horrible it was inside the black fog for all those people in D.C. and Rapid City. What can be done to help survivors?"

"It would be interesting to find out," she said. "Maybe that's something we should get involved with. We're all looking and moving ahead now."

Amy wrapped her arm around Paul's and led him back into the house.

Yeah, Paul thought. *Looking ahead.*

<<< The End >>>

Look for *Nasty Leftovers* by Guy L. Pace.

Reality is back on track, but the world is devastated with only a remnant of humanity left. On a mission to restore Washington, D.C., Paul Shannon and Amy Grossman must face a sinister presence left behind by Satan. In the ensuing battle, physical and spiritual warfare is waged against the possessed, hellhounds, and even the evil presence itself. In this fast-paced sequel to Sudden Mission, can Paul, Amy, and their army of faithful triumph against such impossible odds?

MORE GREAT READS

Freedom's Secret by **Amy McCoy Dees** (YA Historical Christian Fiction) Keegan O'Malley has long since escaped the Jamaican sugar plantation and found freedom in St. Augustine, Florida. He vows to find his brother and childhood friend, his journey leading him through secret tunnels, over rushing rivers, and inside smelly, pirate-filled taverns.

Wheelman by **Brian L. Tucker** (Young Adult) When foster teen Cy Vance discovers his dad–one of the FBI's Most Wanted–is alive and well in Mexico, he must decide how far he'll go to help his family, even if it costs him his life.

The Chronicle of the Three: Bloodline by **Tabitha Caplinger** (Christian Fantasy) When Zoe Andrews discovers she is part of an ancient bloodline, she also learns that not all shadows are harmless interceptions of light. But Zoe, the daughter of the three, isn't just another descendant–she's the key to humanity's salvation.